Suddenly, as if in answer to a prayer, Gaia heard voices behind her. She stopped and fumbled through her backpack as if she were looking for something. Jeez, what a girl had to do to get mugged in this city.

The voices turned into whispers, and then she heard footsteps, slow. Oh, *yes.* Finally. She turned toward the noise, pasting what she hoped looked like a terrified expression on her face. Inside, her heart was leaping with anticipation.

There were three of them, and they looked young—around sixteen or seventeen. Two of them had shaved heads. The smallest brandished a razor blade.

The little thug was up front, covering the ground between them with a menacing lurch. The other two were hanging back, present to witness this feat of loyalty. It was becoming obvious to Gaia what was up here, and it pissed her off.

Come on, boys, she silently encouraged them. *Come and get me.*

FEARLESS™

FRANCINE PASCAL

POCKET PULSE
New York London Toronto Sydney Tokyo Singapore

To my daughters,
Jamie Stewart, Laurie Wenk, Susan Johansson

An *Original* Publication *of* POCKET BOOKS

POCKET PULSE, published by
Pocket Books, a division of Simon & Schuster, Inc.
1230 Avenue of the Americas, New York, NY 10020

Produced by 17th Street Productions, Inc.,
a division of Daniel Weiss Associates, Inc.
33 West 17th Street, New York, NY 10011

Cover photography by St. Denis. Cover design by Mike Rivilis.

ISBN: 0-671-03941-5

First Pocket Pulse Paperback printing October 1999

10 9 8 7 6 5 4 3 2 1

Printed in the U.S.A.

GAIA

Losers with no imagination say that if you start a new school, there has to be a first day. How come they haven't figured out how to beat that? Just think existentially. All you do is take what's supposed to be the first day and bury it someplace in the next month. By the time you get around to it a month later, who cares?

When I first heard the word *existential*, I didn't know what it meant, so I never used it. But then I found out that no one knows what it means, so now I use it all the time.

Since I just moved to New York last week, tomorrow would have been my first day at the new school, but I existentialized it, and now I've got a good thirty days before I have to deal with it. So, like, it'll be just a regular day, and I'll just grab my usual school stuff, jeans and a T-shirt, and throw them on. Then just like I always do, I'll take them off and throw on about eighteen different T-shirts and four different pairs of jeans before I find the right ones that hide my diesel arms and thunder thighs. Not good things on a girl, but no one else seems to see them like I do.

I won't bother to clean up when I'm done. I don't want to trick my new cohabitants, George and Ella, into thinking that I'm neat or considerate or anything. Why set them up for disappointment? I made that mistake with my old cohabitants and . . . well, I'm not living with them anymore, am I?

George Niven was my dad's mentor in the CIA. He's old. Like fifty or something. His wife, Ella, is much younger. Maybe thirty, I don't know. And you certainly can't tell from the way she dresses. Middle of winter she finds a way to show her belly button. And she's got four hundred of these little elastic bands that can only pass for a skirt if you never move your legs. Top that with this unbelievable iridescent red hair and you've got one hot seventeen-year-old. At least that's what she thinks. We all live cozy together in Greenwich Village in a brownstone—that's what they call row houses in New York City. Don't ask me why, because it isn't brown, but we'll let that go for now.

I'm not sure how this transfer of me and my pathetic possessions was arranged. Not by my dad. He is Out of the Picture. No letters. No birthday cards. He didn't even contact me in the hospital last year when I almost fractured my skull. (And no, I didn't almost fracture my skull to test my dad, as a certain asshole suggested.) I haven't seen him since I was twelve, since . . . since—I guess it's time to back up a little. My name is Gaia. Guy. Uh. Yes, it's a weird name. No, I don't feel like explaining it right now.

I am seventeen. The good thing about seventeen is that you're not sixteen. Sixteen goes with the word *sweet*, and I am so far from sweet. I've got a black belt in kung fu and I'm trained in karate, judo, jujitsu, and *muay thai*—which is basically kick boxing. I've got a reflex speed that's off the charts. I'm a near perfect shot. I can climb mountains, box, wrestle, break codes in four languages. I can throw a 175-pound man over my shoulders, which accounts for my disgusting shoulders. I can kick just about anybody's ass. I'm not bragging. I wish I were. I wish my dad hadn't made me into the . . . thing I am.

I have blond hair. Not yellow, fairy-tale blond. But blond enough to stick me in the category. You know, so guys expect you to expect them to hit on you. So teachers set your default grade at B-minus. C-plus if you happen to have big breasts, which I don't particularly. My friend from before, Ivy, had this equation between grades and cup size, but I'll spare you that.

Back in ninth grade I dyed my way right out of the blond category, but after a while it got annoying. The dye stung and turned my hands orange. To be honest, though (and I am not a liar), there's another reason I let my hair grow back. Being blond makes people think they can pick on you, and I like when people think they can pick on me.

You see, I have this handicap. Uh, that's the wrong word. I am hormonally challenged. I am never afraid. I just don't have the gene or whatever it is that makes you scared.

It's not like I'll jump off a cliff or anything. I'm not an idiot. My rationality is not defective. In fact, it's extra good. They say nothing clouds your reason like fear. But then, I wouldn't know. I don't know what it feels like to be scared.

It's like if you don't have hope, how can you imagine it? Or being born blind, how do you know what colors are?

I guess you'd say I'm fearless. Whatever fear is.

If I see some big guy beating up on a little guy, I just dive in and finish him off. And I can. Because that's the way I've been trained. I'm so strong, you wouldn't believe. But I hate it.

Since I'm never afraid of anything, my dad figured he'd better make sure I can hold my own when I rush into things. What he did really worked, too. Better than he expected. See, my dad didn't consider nature.

Nature compensates for its mistakes. If it forgot to give me a fear gene, it gave me some other fantastic abilities that definitely work in my favor. When I need it, I have this awesome speed, enormous energy, and amazing strength all quadrupled because there's no fear to hold me back.

It's even hard for me to figure out. People talk about danger and being careful. In my head I totally understand, but in my gut I just don't feel it. So if I see somebody in trouble, I just jump in and use everything I've got. And that's big stuff, and it's intense.

I mean, you ever hear that story about the mother who lifted the car off her little boy? That's like the kind of strength regular people can get from adrenaline. Except I don't need extra adrenaline because without fear, there's nothing to stop you from using every bit of power you have.

And a human body, especially a highly trained one like mine, has a lot of concentrated power.

But there's a price. I remember once reading about the Spartans. They were these fantastic Greek warriors about four hundred something B.C. They beat everybody. Nobody could touch them. But after a battle they'd get so drained, they'd shake all over and practically slide to the ground. That's what happens to me. It's like I use up everything and my body gets really weak and I almost black out. But it only lasts a couple of minutes. Eventually I'm okay again.

And there is one other thing that works in my favor. I can do whatever I want 'cause I've got nothing to lose.

See, my mother is . . . not here anymore. I don't really care that my dad is gone because I hate his guts. I don't have any brothers or sisters. I don't even have any grandparents. Well, actually, I think I do have one, but she lives in some end-of-the-world place in Russia and I get the feeling she's a few beans short of a burrito. But this is a tangent.

Tangent is a heinous word for two reasons:

1. It appears in my trigonometry book.

2. Ella, the woman-with-whom-I-now-live-never-to-be-confused-with-a-mother, accuses me of "going off on them."

Where was I? Right. I was telling you my secrets. It probably all boils down to three magic words: I don't care. I have no family, pets, or friends. I don't even have a lamp or a pair of pants I give a shit about.

I Don't Care.

And nobody can make me.

Ella says I'm looking for trouble. For a dummy she hit it right this time.

I *am* looking for trouble.

He lay
sprawled in
a half-
conscious
pile, and
she was
tempted to
demand his
wallet or
his watch or
something.

a walking trap

The Point

DON'T GO INTO THE PARK AFTER sunset. The warning rolled around Gaia Moore's head as she crossed the street that bordered Washington Square Park to the east. She savored the words as she would a forkful of chocolate cheesecake.

There was a stand of trees directly in front of her and a park entrance a couple hundred feet to the left. She hooked through the trees, feeling the familiar fizz in her limbs. It wasn't fear, of course. It was energy, maybe even excitement—the things that came when fear should have. She passed slowly through a grassy stretch, staying off the lighted paths that snaked inefficiently through the park.

As the crow flies. That's how she liked to walk. So what if she had nowhere to go? So what if no one on earth knew or probably cared where she was or when she'd get home? That wasn't the point. It didn't mean she had to take the long way. She was starting a new school in the morning, and she meant to put as much distance between herself and tomorrow as she could. Walking fast didn't stop the earth's slow roll, but sometimes it felt like it could.

She'd passed the midway point, marked by the miniature Arc de Triomph, before she caught the flutter of a shadow out of the corner of her eye. She didn't turn her head. She hunched her shoulders so her tall frame looked smaller. The shadow froze. She could feel eyes on her back. Bingo.

The mayor liked to brag how far the New York City crime rate had fallen, but Washington Square at night didn't disappoint. In her short time here she'd learned it was full of junkies who couldn't resist a blond girl with a full wallet, especially under the cover of night.

Gaia didn't alter the rhythm of her steps. An attacker proceeded differently when he sensed your awareness. Any deception was her advantage.

The energy was building in her veins. Come on, she urged silently. Her mind was beautifully blank. Her concentration was perfect. Her ears were pricked to decipher the subtlest motion.

Yet she could have sensed the clumsy attacker thundering from the brush if she'd been deaf and blind. A heavy arm was thrown over her shoulders and tightened around her neck.

"Oh, please," she muttered, burying an elbow in his solar plexus.

As he staggered backward and sucked for air, she turned on him indignantly. Yes, it was a big, clumsy, stupid him—a little taller than average and young, probably not even twenty years old. She felt a tiny spark of hope as she let her eyes wander through the bushes. Maybe there were more . . . ? The really incompetent dopes usually traveled in packs. But she heard nothing more than his noisy, X-rated complaints.

She let him come at her again. Might as well get a shred of a workout. She even let him earn a little speed as he barreled toward her. She loved turning a man's own strength against him. That was the essence of it. She reversed his momentum with a fast knee strike and finished him off with a front kick.

He lay sprawled in a half-conscious pile, and she was tempted to demand his wallet or his watch or something. A smile flickered over her face. It would be amusing, but that wasn't the point, was it?

Just as she was turning away, she detected a faint glitter on the ground near his left arm. She came closer and leaned down. It was a razor blade, shiny but not perfectly clean. In the dark she couldn't tell if the crud on the blade was rust or blood. She glanced quickly at her hands. No, he'd done her no harm. But it lodged in her mind as a strange choice of weapon.

She walked away without bothering to look further. She knew he'd be fine. Her specialty was subduing without causing any real damage. He'd lie there for a few minutes. He'd be sore, maybe bruised tomorrow. He'd brush the cobwebs off his imagination to invent a story for his buddies about how three seven-foot, three-hundred-pound male karate black belts attacked him in the park.

But she would bet her life on the fact that he would never sneak up on another fragile-looking woman without remembering this night. And that was the point. That was what Gaia lived for.

An Easy Crowd

"WHO CAN COME TO THE BOARD AND write out the quadratic formula?" Silence.

"A volunteer, please? I need a volunteer."

No. Gaia sent the teacher telepathic missiles. *Do not call on me.*

"Come on, kids. This is basic stuff. You are supposed to be the advanced class. Am I in the wrong room?"

The teacher's voice—what was the woman's name again?—was reedy and awful sounding. Gaia really should have remembered the name, considering this *was not* the first day.

No. No. No. The teacher's eyes swept over the second-to-back row twice before they rested on Gaia. *Shit.*

"You, in the . . . brown, is it? What's your name?"

"Gaia."

"Gay what?"

Every member of the class snickered.

The beautiful thing about Gaia was that she didn't hate them for laughing. In fact, she loved them for being so predictable. It made them so manageable. There was nothing those buttheads could give that Gaia couldn't take.

"Guy. (Pause) Uh."

The teacher cocked her head as if the name were some kind of insult. "Right, then. Come on up to the board. Guy (pause) uh."

The class snickered again.

God, she hated school. Gaia dragged herself out of her chair. Why was she here, anyway? She didn't want to be a doctor or a lawyer. She didn't want to be a CIA agent or Green Beret or superoperative *X-Files* type, like her dad had obviously hoped.

What did she want to be when she grew up? (She loved that question.) A waitress. She wanted to serve food at some piece-of-crap greasy spoon and wait for a customer to bitch her out, or stiff her on the tip, or PINCH HER BUTT. She'd travel across the country from one bad restaurant to the next and scare people who thought it was okay to be mean to waitresses. And there were a lot of people like that. Nobody got more shit than a waitress did. (Well, maybe telemarketers, but they sort of deserved it.)

"Gaia? Any day now."

Snicker. Snicker. This was an easy crowd. Ms.

What's-her-face must have been thrilled with her success.

Gaia hesitated at the board for a moment.

"You don't know it, do you?" The teacher's tone was possibly the most patronizing thing she had ever heard.

Gaia didn't answer. She just wrote the formula out very slowly, appreciating the horrible grinding screech of the chalk as she drew the equals sign. It sounded a lot like the teacher's voice, actually.

$$x = \frac{-b \pm \sqrt{b^2 - 4ac}}{2a}$$

At the last second she changed the final plus to a minus sign. Of course she knew the formula. What was she, stupid? Her dad had raced her through basic algebra by third grade. She'd (begrudgingly) mastered multivariable calculus and linear algebra before she started high school. She might hate math, but she was good at it.

"I'm sorry, Gaia. That's incorrect. You may sit down."

Gaia tried to look disappointed as she shuffled to her chair.

"Talk to me after class about placement, please." The teacher said that in a slightly lower voice, as if the rest of the students wouldn't hear she found Gaia unfit for the class. "Yes, ma'am," Gaia said brightly. It was the first ray of light all day. She'd demote herself to memorizing times tables if it meant getting a different teacher.

Times tables actually came in pretty handy for a waitress. What with figuring out tips and all.

Not Cloying

HE SAW HER RIGHT AFTER THE seventh-period bell rang. She seemed dressed for the sole purpose of blending in with the lockers, but she stood out, anyway. It didn't matter that her wide blue eyes were narrowed or that her pretty mouth was twisted into a near snarl—she was blatantly beautiful. It was kind of sick the way Ed was preoccupied with beautiful girls these days.

There weren't many people left in the hall at this point. He, of course, had permission to take his own sweet time getting to class. And she was probably lost. She cast him a quick glance as she strode down the hall. The kind of glance where she saw him without actually seeing him. He was used to that.

He felt a little sorry for her. (He was also preoccupied

with finding ways of feeling sorry for people.) She was new and trying hard not to look it. She was confused and trying to look tough. It was endearing is what it was.

"Hey, can I help you find a classroom or anything?"

She swiveled around and glared at him like he'd made a lewd remark. (Was she some kind of mind reader?)

"Excuse me?" she demanded. She wasn't afraid to give him a good once-over.

"You look lost," he explained.

Now she was angry. "This is not what lost looks like. This is what annoyed looks like. And no, I don't need any help. Thanks."

It was the spikiest, least gracious "thanks" he'd ever heard. "Anytime," he said, trying not to smile. "So, what's your name?"

"Does it matter?" She couldn't believe he was prolonging the conversation.

"Mine's Ed, by the way."

"I'm so happy for you." She gave him an extra snarl before she bolted down the hall to the science wing.

He smiled all the way to physics class. He almost laughed out loud when he passed through the door and saw her shadowy, hunched-over form casting around for a seat in the back.

She was in his class; this was excellent. Maybe she'd call him a name if he struck up another conversation.

Even curse him out. That might be fun. God, he'd probably earn himself a restraining order if he tried to sit next to her.

He was so tired of saccharine smiles and cloying tones of voice. People always plastered their eyes to his face for fear of looking anywhere else. He was fed up with everybody being so goddamned nice.

That's why he'd already fallen in love with this weird, maladjusted, beautiful girl who carried a chip the size of Ohio on her shoulder. Because nobody was ever mean to the guy in the wheelchair.

September 23

My Dearest Gaia,

I saw a mouse race across the floor of my apartment today, and it made me think of you. (What doesn't make me think of you?) It reminded me of the winter of Jonathan and your secret efforts to save his little life. I never imagined I'd think longingly upon an oversized gray field mouse whose contribution to our lives was a thousand turds on the kitchen counter, but I grew to love him almost as much as you did.

Oh, Gaia. It feels as if it's been so long. Do you still love rodents and other despised creatures? Do you still carry a pocket full of pennies for luck? Do you still eat your cereal without milk? Do you ever think about me anymore?

I write it and think it so often, it's a mantra, but

Gaia, how desperately I hope you'll forgive me someday. You'll understand why I did what I did, and you'll know it was because I love you. I have so many doubts and fears, my darling, and they seem to grow as the days between us pass. But I know I love you. I'd give my life for you. Again.

Tom Moore lifted his pen at the sound of the beeper. God, he hated that sound. He didn't need to look at the readout to know who was summoning him. It wasn't as if he had friends and family swarming about—it was his self-inflicted punishment that if he couldn't be with his daughter, he would be alone.

He snatched the wretched little device from his desk and threw it across the room, mildly amazed at his own rare show of temper as the beeper bounced off the windowsill and skittered across the wood floor. It was always the same people. It was always an emergency. By tomorrow he'd be in a different time zone.

Before he picked up the phone, he walked to the ancient aluminum filing cabinet and opened it. He thumbed through the files without needing to look. Locating the thick pile of papers, he placed the letter at the front, just as he always did with all the others, unsent and locked in the drawer.

[illegible] Doctor. I hope you'll forgive me someday [illegible] and understand why I did what I did, and you'll know it wasn't because I don't care. I know so many students and [illegible] darlings, and they were [illegible] [illegible] to pass. But I know? [illegible] [illegible] you again.

Tom Moore lifted his pen at the sound of the beeper. God, he hated that sound. He didn't need to look at the readout to know who was summoning him. It wasn't as if he had friends and family waiting about—it was his self-inflicted punishment that if he couldn't be with his daughter, he would be alone.

He snatched the oversized little beeper from the desk and threw it across the room, mildly amused at his own fine show of temper as the beeper bounced off the wood wall and skittered across the wood floor. It was always the same people. It was always an emergency. By tomorrow he'd be in a different time zone.

Before he picked up the phone, he walked to the ancient aluminum filing cabinet and opened it. He thumbed through the files without needing to look. Locating the thick file of papers, he placed the letter at the front, just as he always did with all the others unread and locked in the drawer.

MacDougal and
LaGuardia—
bzzzt—slashing
victim, female
African American
in her
thirties—
bzzzt—
young male
perpetrator—
bzzzz . . .

a stupid hobby

"HELLO, CEEENDY."

"Hi, Zolov. What's shaking?"

"Shakeeeng?"

Her Favorite Place

Gaia laughed. "How are you playing?"

Zolov worked his mouth. He drew his wrinkly brown hand over his lips, thinking about the question seriously. "I beat everyone."

"Of course you did," Gaia said loudly. "You're the best."

He nodded absently. "Tank you. You are a good geerl."

In spite of the fact she was practically shouting at him, Gaia could tell he was reading her lips and that it was tiring for him. He sat back in the sunshine, ready for his next opponent, who would very likely not show. His favorite chessboard was set. As always, it was presided over by one of the Mighty Morphin Power Rangers, a red, helmeted action figure he'd probably picked up in somebody's garbage. He never played without him.

Gaia would have sat down across from him if she'd had more than twenty cents in her pocket. Instead she lay back on the bench and closed her eyes.

This park, these chess tables, was Gaia's favorite place. It was her home in New York more than George and Ella's house ever would be. Zolov was at least ninety years old and thought her name was Cindy, but even so, he was her favorite person.

Who says I have no life? she mused as she stretched her arms behind her head, feeling the fabric of her gray T-shirt creeping over her belly button. She inhaled the scent of sugary nuts roasting in a pushcart nearby. This was her favorite place, and that was her favorite smell. It was so sweet and strong, she could practically taste it. One of these days she was going to buy a big bag of those nuts and scarf them down without even pausing to breathe.

She felt a shadow come over her face and squinted one eye open. "Hey, Renny," she said. "You ready for 'dimes of demonstration'?"

Renny was a thirteen-year-old Puerto Rican boy—Gaia's second-favorite person. He was a self-proclaimed poet and such a whiz at chess he hustled great sums of money out of almost anybody who was dumb enough to sit down across from him. Today his face didn't light up with its usual bravado.

Gaia sat up and put a hand over her eyes to block the sun. "You're scared I'm going to steal your money and make you cry?" she taunted. She scanned the tables for a free board.

As she did, her eye snagged on a new piece of graffiti splayed on the asphalt just to the left of Zolov's usual table. A swastika. It was at least a foot across, and the white paint was as fresh and bright as a new pair of sneakers. Gaia's stomach was filled with lead. Could it be for her benefit? she wondered. Could somebody possibly know how the Holocaust had decimated her mother's family and made her grandparents into heroes? No. Not likely. She was being paranoid. How would anyone know about her Jewish background? In fact, when she told some people, they acted all surprised—like if you had fair hair and blue eyes, it wasn't possible. That really annoyed her.

Her eyes flicked over the ugly shape again. Had Renny seen it? Had Zolov? Did they think anything of it?

For some reason Renny wasn't jumping in with his usual rhyming insults and eager put-downs.

"Gaia, you oughtta go home," Renny said almost inaudibly in the direction of his sneakers.

This was odd. "What's up, Renny?"

"It's gonna get dark," he noted.

"Thanks, Ren. It usually does." He was wearing a stiff new jacket that advertised its brand name from three different spots. He licked his lips. "You oughtta, you know, be watching out," he continued.

"For what?" she asked.

He considered this question a moment. "The park is real dangerous after dark."

Gaia stood, impatient. She swept a strand of hair behind her ear. "Renny, cut the bullshit. What's the matter? What are you talking about?"

"Did you hear about Lacy's sister?" His face was slightly pink, and he wasn't meeting her gaze.

"No, why?"

"It was on the news and everything. All the kids are talking about it. She got slashed in the park last night," Renny explained. "She had to get sewn up from her eyebrow to her ear."

"God, that's awful," Gaia said. "What kind of blade?"

"What?"

"What kind of blade?"

Renny gave her a strange look.

"Was it a razor blade?" Gaia persisted.

"I guess. I don't know." He looked up at her a little defiantly. "How am I supposed to know?"

"Just asking, Renny." She softened her tone. "Thanks for warning me. I do appreciate it."

He nodded, his face growing pinker. "I was just . . . you know, concerned about you." He tried to look very tall as he shuffled away.

Gaia swung her beat-up messenger bag over her shoulder as she watched him. She had a bad feeling about this. She sensed that Renny was no longer satisfied with the insular world of chess misfits. He was starting to care what the big boys thought—those stupid boys who hung around the fountain, trying to look tough. Renny was smarter and funnier and more original than they'd ever be, but he was thirteen. He was at that brutal age when many kids would sell all the uniqueness in their character for the right pair of shoes. She longed to tell him not to spend so much time in the park, to go home to his mother, but who was she to talk?

Yes, Renny might be concerned about her. But not as concerned as she was about him.

She herself loved this misfit world, Gaia mused as she surveyed the tables. Curtis, a fifteen-year-old black kid, was sitting across from Mr. Haq, a Pakistani taxicab driver who appeared to like nothing more than parking his yellow cab on Washington Square South and killing an afternoon over a chessboard.

She loved that people who couldn't begin to pronounce each other's names played and talked for hours. She loved that a forty-something-year-old cabdriver and a fifteen-year-old from the Manhattan Valley youth program had so much in common. She loved getting a break from the stupid hierarchy of high school.

She loved that there weren't people like . . . well, people like . . . him.

The him was walking by slowly, looking confidently over the boards in play. His hair was light in color—a tousled mixture of blond and brown and even a little red. His chinos were cuffed, and his preppy gray jacket flapped in the autumn breeze. Gaia felt her stomach do a quick pitch and roll. She felt queasy and strangely alert at the same time.

You didn't find people who looked like that . . . as in, stunningly, astonishingly good. People like him sipped coffee at Dean & Deluca or swing danced on Gap commercials or spouted Woody Allen–style dialogue on *Dawson's Creek,* where they belonged.

So what *the hell* was he doing lingering over chessboards with the freaks and geeks? She had half a mind to walk right over and tell him to get lost.

This was her favorite place, and he had no business here, reminding her of things she would never be.

Don't Be Afraid

"Thank you, Marco, you're a sweetheart."

Marco nodded at the woman, making sure to tilt his chin so she had a good look at his left side, the side where his broken nose hardly showed at all. "No problem." He kept his voice deep and smooth. She probably thought he was like twenty-five or something.

She took a long sip from the bottle of Coke he'd brought her, exposing her pale neck. She lifted one leg to rest on the low wall of the fountain, revealing several more inches of thigh under her stretchy aqua miniskirt. He tried not to stare. Or did she want him to stare?

He stopped breathing completely as she slowly, slowly brushed her fingers over his upper arm. "What happened here?" she asked.

He glanced at the purplish bruise. He paused before answering and cleared his throat, trying to make certain his voice didn't come out squeaky. "Nothing much. I got jumped last night. These three big guys thought they were real tough. Probably black belts in karate or something."

Her eyes widened in just the way he'd hoped. "You're okay? Did you call the police?"

"Uh-uh. That's not how we—how I—do things." Marco ran a hand through his dark hair. It had come out perfectly today. "I've got some friends who will back me up if those guys ever come back here." Marco loved the way she watched him when he talked. So he kept talking. He wasn't even listening to what he was saying.

Man, she was gorgeous. She was older than he, twenty-something at least, but sexy as hell. Like some kind of goddess with her straight red hair and green eyes. And the legs on her. He couldn't look away.

He'd first noticed her at the beginning of the summer. All the guys noticed her—it was hard not to. She lived around here, he guessed, because she walked by this fountain almost every afternoon. He wasn't the only one who magically turned up each day around four o'clock to watch the show.

Lately he'd noticed she'd started returning his looks. Just a glance at first, but then her eyes stayed longer. Last week she'd said hello to him, and he'd practically peed in his pants. Today she'd been late, so most of the guys had wandered away, but some kind of crazy instinct made him stay.

He took his eyes off her breasts for a moment to see if he spotted anybody he knew. He would love for any one of his buddies to see him right now.

Just then she reached toward his collarbone and rested her index finger on the pendant that lay there. The electricity from her touch surged through his chest and seemed to throw his heart off rhythm. "What is this?" Her voice was almost a whisper. "I've seen this before."

He studied her face before he answered. He wasn't sure how much to tell—how much she really wanted to know. "It's, uh, it's called a hieroglyph—you know, like ancient Egyptian writing? It's the symbol for . . . uh, power."

"Where have I seen it before?" Her green eyes fixed on his.

His glance darted around the fountain. "I don't know. Maybe you saw one of the other guys wearing it. Maybe a tattoo on somebody's arm. It's kind of a . . . I don't know . . . kind of a . . ."

His voice trailed off awkwardly. He didn't want her thinking he was some kind of thug. He sure didn't want anybody to overhear him telling her secret stuff.

"A mark?" she supplied. "Some sort of identification?" She didn't appear wary the way most girls he knew would. Her eyes were wide and intense, fascinated.

"Yeah, like that."

"Ah. I see. Are you part of—"

Marco sucked in his breath. Suddenly this didn't seem so cool. What if she was an undercover cop or some kind of informer? He'd heard of stuff like this. He backed up, putting a few feet between them. "I gotta be going. It's, like, after six, and I—"

With two steps she closed the distance. "Marco. Don't be afraid of me." Her fingers fluttered over his cheek. "Don't tell me anything you don't want to. I'm just . . . interested, that's all. I'm interested in everything about you."

All the blood in his body seemed to pool in his

head. He felt dizzy. "You're not, like, a cop or anything?" He was pretty sure she'd have to say so if she were.

She laughed. "No. Most definitely not." She gave him a look. It was a mischievous, sexy kind of look. "*Definitely* not."

Rapunzel Monkey

GAIA SMACKED THE SHORTWAVE RADIO that sat on the table next to the bed. Her bed. She had trouble thinking of anything in this house as hers.

"Piece of crap," she murmured. She'd picked up the radio at a junk shop on Canal Street. She'd gotten it to tune in to the local police frequency, but the damn thing emitted almost nothing but static. She rearranged the antenna she'd rigged until she heard a break in the fuzz. She rolled off the bed and walked to the window. Ah, that was good. She could decipher various bleeps that sounded almost like words. She stood by the door. Oh, it liked that. Now she could actually understand the words.

Bzzzzt—MacDougal and LaGuardia—*bzzzt*—slashing

victim, female African American in her thirties—*bzzzt*—young male perpetrator—*bzzzz* . . .

Dammit. She tried jumping up and down.

—lost him in the park—*bzzzzzzzz* . . .

Shit. Gaia grabbed the radio and threw it off the table. What a stupid hobby. Why couldn't she just watch *Roswell* like a normal girl?

Well, for one thing, because the television was in the so-called family room. It would mean walking past, possibly even fraternizing with, George and his bimbo bride. It wasn't that she didn't like George. She did. He was trying really hard to make her feel comfortable. He tried so hard, in fact, that she found it awkward to be around him. He put on this peppy voice and asked her about her classes or her friends. What was she going to say, "I see my math teacher through crosshairs"? "My best friend has Alzheimer's"? George wanted something within the universe of normal, and she simply couldn't give him that.

Ella was another story. Stupid, vain Ella she genuinely disliked. There were Ella's fingernails, her passion for Victoria's Secret catalogs, her love of Mariah Carey. That was about it for Ella. How in the world had a sensible man like George fallen prey to a tarty thing like her? And God, he had fallen.

Gaia really needed some air. She strode to the door

of the room and listened for signs of life. What sucked was that her room was on the fourth floor of the four-story house. She hid up there during the little time she spent in the house because she hated walking past every other room on her way in and out. She was like a latter-day Rapunzel except her hair was only a few inches below her shoulders, slightly fried, not all that blond, and furthermore, who the hell was ever going to climb up to give her a hand? The guy in the wheel-chair from school?

What she—and Rapunzel, frankly—needed was a decent ladder.

Gaia opened the door slowly. Hopefully George was still at work and Ella was—who ever knew where Ella was? By profession Ella considered herself a photographer, but Gaia had a hard time taking her seriously. It gave Ella an excuse to saunter through hip downtown neighborhoods with a camera slung over her shoulder. Apparently she got the odd commission to photograph somebody's dog or living room or something. Her "work," as George called it in his pious way, was displayed over most of the wall space in the house—mostly arty black-and-white pictures of dolls' heads and high-heeled shoes.

Thank God for the automatic camera that makes it all possible, Gaia thought sarcastically as she crept through the hallway and down the stairs.

At the second landing she was faced once again

by "the photograph." Most days she averted her eyes. Although Ella hadn't taken it, it was by far the most upsetting in the house. It was a picture of an eleven-year-old Gaia with her parents, snapped by George the week he visited them at their country house in the Berkshires. Once Gaia looked at the photo, she found it hard to look away and, after that, hard to get her mind to cooperate with her.

The Gaia in the picture made her think of a little monkey, clinging to her dad with long skinny arms, her wrists circled by several filthy friendship bracelets, her narrow shoulders lost in the beloved brown fisherman's sweater he'd bought for her on a trip to Ireland. Gaia's smile was big and exuberant, so pitifully unaware of what the next year would bring.

Now Gaia moved her gaze to her mother, even as she willed herself not to. If Gaia's face in the picture was all embarrassing openness, her mother's was pure mystery. No matter how many times Gaia searched it, no matter how clearly she saw those features, she felt she couldn't tell what her mother really looked like. She *needed* something from that face that it never gave. The same miserable questions started their spiraling march through Gaia's brain: *Why am I holding Daddy and not you? Why aren't I beautiful like you? Did you love me, anyway? Did you ever know how much I loved you?*

And then, as always, the thoughts got so unfathomably sad, they didn't even come in words. Her throat started to ache, and her vision swam. She couldn't pull enough air into her lungs. Without exactly realizing what she was doing, her hands shot out and yanked the framed photograph off the wall.

"What are you doing?"

Gaia spun around. Her heart was bouncing in her chest, and it took her a moment to focus her eyes on Ella. She cleared her throat. She took a deep breath. She tried to rearrange her posture into something less rigid.

"I am removing this picture from the wall."

"Can I ask why?"

"Sure."

Ella waited impatiently. "Okay, why?"

Gaia placed the picture facedown on the bookcase. She glanced at her watch. "I didn't say I'd answer."

Ella got that eye-rolling martyred look. "Gaia, you know George loves that picture. He put it up for you."

Gaia cleared her throat again. She tried shrugging, but it didn't come off with the indifference she was aiming for. "If George put it up for my benefit, he won't mind if I take it down."

Ella's hands found their way to her hips as they mostly did within a few minutes of starting a conversation with Gaia. "I swear, Gaia, George does so much for you. I would think you could at least—"

Gaia tuned out the shrill voice as she made her way

down the rest of the steps and out the front door. She knew every word of the speech. There wouldn't be any vocabulary words or clever turns of phrase. Ella wasn't going to surprise her.

Gaia took the sidewalk at a near run. She felt like she might explode. The sky was darkening as she turned left on West 4th Street, leaving bustling outdoor cafes, overpriced little restaurants, all-night delis, her favorite subterranean record shop behind her in a blur.

She headed straight for the park. No one was going to scare her out of her shortcut. And certainly not tonight, not in the mood she was in. And in fact, she hoped they'd try. Let them find her instead of some kid or some old guy who wouldn't know how to handle it. Maybe if she did this enough, those creeps would learn that everyone who looked vulnerable wasn't necessarily so. What a gorgeous lesson to teach them. After all, wasn't that what her gifts were all about? Power to the little people!

She spun
around,
instantly
accosted by
strange
blurred
images.
A flash of
chrome. Two
large
wheels.

mr.
valiant

A Force for Good

THREE MORE STEPS. OKAY, FIVE MORE steps. Okay, ten more. Just to the maple tree. Okay, not that one, the one behind it.

She was a little nuts. She knew it. Skulking around Washington Square Park for three hours and twenty-three minutes, counting steps (and okay, seconds), looking for trouble. It could be called entrapment. That's exactly what she wanted to do, entrap those lowlifes.

Gaia lingered under the tree, feeling drops of sweat sliding down her spine. Wasn't New York City supposed to be getting cool in September? The smell of late season pollen was so thick, it felt like paste in her nostrils. Please, somebody. Anybody. She'd come here with the secret hope that one of the notorious slashers would have a go at her, but now she'd grown desperate. She would take absolutely any criminal, from petty shoplifter to ax murderer; she really wasn't choosy. Hey, who even needed a criminal? She was ready to pounce on the strength of a big mouth or a bad attitude.

But she wouldn't. Gaia would never attack anybody unprovoked. She would never do more harm than necessary. That was the code, and as much as she hated her father, she was still bound to honor it. It was bred into her, just like her blue eyes that seemed to change shade with her mood, the weather, the color of her shirt. Just like her love of sweets. She had to use her Miraculous Gift (that's what her father always called it) as a force for good. Her mission was to draw out violent behavior and squash it, not to produce more violence.

But sometimes carrying out her mission felt more self-indulgent than honorable. `Did it count as a good deed if you enjoyed yourself?` She liked to think she thrived on self-defense. But there were times, really upsetting times, when she saw the line between defense and offense as clear as day and barreled toward it. Hey, she had an extraordinary talent, and she wanted to use it.

What if one day she crossed that line that separated good guys from bad guys? `It would be easy.` There was only a hair's width between them. Why hadn't anyone warned her that inside the crucible of real anger, good and bad were so nearly the same?

Worse yet, what if one day she'd stop being able to see the line at all? She wouldn't know anymore if she was good or bad or crazy or sane. Maybe Gaia didn't know the meaning of scary, but that sounded an awful lot like it.

Gaia made a slow loop around the maple tree. She had to get out of this park, but she really didn't feel like going back to George and Ella's. God forbid

George would put on that earnest face and try to talk about "her loss" as he often did after Ella complained about her.

She didn't feel like walking on Broadway—the street was mobbed with NYU students, tourists, and shoppers at every hour of the day. Instead she turned south on Mercer Street. She loved the deserted, canyonlike feel of the narrow street and the sound her steps made on the cobblestones. She'd walk straight down to Houston Street and see what was playing at the Angelika.

Suddenly, as if in answer to a prayer, Gaia heard voices behind her. She stopped and fumbled through her backpack as if she were looking for something. Jeez, what a girl had to do to get mugged in this city.

The voices turned into whispers, and then she heard footsteps, slow. Oh, *yes.* Finally. She turned toward the noise, pasting what she hoped looked like a terrified expression on her face. Inside, her heart was leaping with anticipation.

There were three of them, and they looked young—around sixteen or seventeen. Two of them had shaved heads. The smallest brandished a razor blade. Gaia detected more than a hint of nervousness under his swagger. She backed up (fearfully, she hoped), wanting the situation to escalate. She hated herself, but there it was.

The little thug was up front, covering the ground

between them with a menacing lurch. The other two were hanging back, present to witness this feat of loyalty. It was becoming obvious to Gaia what was up here, and it pissed her off.

Come on, boys, she silently encouraged them. *Come and get me.* Her mind hovered on the swastika she'd seen painted on the ground in the park. That coupled with the shaved heads and the leather jackets gave her the strong suspicion that these assholes were some kind of neo-Nazi white supremacist outfit.

Her concentration was so keen, she had to remind herself to keep breathing. She couldn't let her anger get the best of her. She had to play this just right. If she struck back too quickly, she might scare them away. The kid was trying hard to look tough, but his toughness went about as deep as the sheen of sweat on his upper lip.

Now. He was right on her, razor blade lifted. She screamed helplessly as she drew back her arm for a sharp blow to his wrist. And just as she balanced her weight to deliver the strike she heard a thunderous shout and a commotion behind her.

Suddenly noise was coming from every direction. Her adrenaline was rising fast, but her focus was thrown. She spun around, instantly accosted by strange blurred images. A flash of chrome. Two large wheels. She jumped back to try to make sense of it.

"Get away from her!" a familiar voice shouted.

Gaia's razor-blade-wielding attacker fell back in confusion.

Equally confused, Gaia swiveled her head.

"It's okay, Gaia! Go! Run!"

She watched in perfect amazement as Ed, the guy in the wheelchair from school, rolled into the fray. Her very own knight in shining armor come to save the day.

"You've got to be joking," she muttered under her breath.

But no, there he was. Mr. Valiant.

Now what was she supposed to do? She couldn't just burst into action with Ed sitting on the sidelines. He'd see everything. He'd know far more than he was allowed.

It was one thing showing an attacker her tricks. Every time she did this, she made a wager that her attacker wouldn't confess to being `pounded by a girl`, and she'd never been wrong. But Ed was a different story. Ed would tell the nifty adventure to everybody in school. They'd probably recruit her for the judo club or something.

The adrenaline was surging through her veins, and the primary person she wanted to strangle was Ed.

The three attackers had been as surprised as she by Ed's arrival, but they were now regrouping.

Okay, fine. She'd take a couple of hits. She wouldn't

let the razor blade near her, but that would be easy enough to dispose of in a stealthy way. They'd hit her. She'd scream. Somebody would hear the noise and call the cops. The three losers would feel manly and dangerous and go away. The little one would earn his initiation on somebody else.

It was disappointing as hell, but she'd deal.

One Small Problem

ED FARGO PUSHED HIS WHEELS AS fast as he could. He sailed over the curb and bumped along the cobblestones. He'd often dreamed of running over somebody with his wheelchair, but he'd never actually done it before. His lungs ached for air and his arms ached with exertion as he plowed through the low bushes and into the guy with the razor blade. Thank God he'd been coming along Mercer just then. Thank God he'd heard the scream.

He heard the powerful meeting of metal and shin bone.

"Ahhhhhhh!" The attacker fell backward.

"Gaia, get out of here!" Ed shouted again. He'd never felt quite so important in his life.

She looked stunned. Why the hell wouldn't she get her ass out of there? Was she paralyzed with fear? So traumatized, she couldn't move a muscle? Thank God he'd arrived when he had. "Please go!" he commanded.

The guy with the razor blade fumbled back up to his feet, and his two accomplices came closer in for backup. Ed realized he didn't have much time. Panic was taking hold of his chest. He looked at Gaia's frozen form. He looked at the three hoods gathering for attack. Oh, man. This time their vicious eyes weren't focused on Gaia; they were aiming directly at him. Oh, oh, oh.

His brain was spinning. His heart was pounding at least five hundred times a minute. The obvious thing to do was get out of there as fast as his arms would carry him, but he couldn't. He couldn't just leave Gaia standing there. She'd be slaughtered.

"What is wrong with you?" Ed bellowed at her. "Get the hell out of here *now!*"

Three big angry thugs were closing in and that stupid girl wouldn't move. Panic was now weirdly tinged with resignation. He was dead. If they wanted to kill him, that is. Maybe they'd be satisfied just mangling him or slashing him to ribbons.

The biggest of the three took hold of the armrest of his wheelchair and gave it a powerful shove. Ed collided hard with the street and rolled from the toppled chair.

This was sad. It sure would have been handy if his legs worked right now. He looked up at the stripe of night sky between the old cast-iron buildings, waiting for the first blow. He put his arms over his face for protection.

Slam! He heard the sound of a foot connecting with hard flesh and then a deep moan. Was that him? Had he made that noise? He heard another searing blow. Jesus, was he so far gone, he couldn't even feel the pain?

He moved an arm away from his face and cracked open one eye. He heard a groan and then a barking shout. Strange. He was pretty sure his mouth was shut. He opened the other eye and sat up. Then he shut both eyes again. Had he gone into cardiac arrest and died already? God, that was quick. Weren't there supposed to be a lot of warm feelings and long tunnels and a bright light?

He simply could not have seen what he thought he saw. He was dead. Or hallucinating. Maybe that was it. His mind was dealing him some truly mind-bending hallucinations. Awesome ones, as it happened. He opened his eyes again. His mouth dropped open.

Gaia Moore, the lovely girl with the slim frame and sullen expression who haunted the back of his physics class, had suddenly transformed into Xena, Warrior Princess, only blond and even more beautiful. She crushed the jaw of Thug 1 with a roundhouse kick.

She struck Thug 2 in the chest with such violence, he was left gasping for breath. Thug 3 came swinging at her from behind, and she spun around and neutralized him with a stunning kick-boxing move he'd only ever seen executed by Jean Claude Van Damme.

Holy shit. Could this actually be real? Gaia's dauntless, intense, angry face looked real. The thonk of her sneakered foot in Thug 1's belly sounded real.

Unbelievable. Gaia was a superhero. Hair flying, limbs whirling, she was the most graceful, powerful martial artist he had ever laid eyes on. Her every move was a mesmerizing combination of ballet and kung fu. And not only was she magical, she was lethal. Thug 1 was writhing on the ground, Thug 2 was ready to flee. Although Thug 3 appeared to be rallying, Ed almost pitied him.

Suddenly Ed sucked in the moist night air. A chill began in his fingertips and crept up his wrists and arms. He saw only a flash at first, and then the image resolved itself. Thug 3 had a knife. Ed saw it clearly now glinting in the streetlight, looking awfully real.

Oh, my God.

Did Gaia see the knife? Did she realize what was coming? He certainly couldn't tell by her expression. Her eyes revealed not even the tiniest hint of fear. Jesus, she was tough. That or paranormally stupid.

"Gaia!" he heard his own voice bellowing. "He's got a knife!"

Her gaze didn't flicker. She stood there motionless as Thug 3 went after her. She looked as if she were in some kind of deep meditation.

Ed was hyperventilating. He didn't care how tough Gaia was; she couldn't defend herself against an eight-inch blade. Presumably her skin was made of the same stuff his was. He had to do something.

He supplied his seizing brain with some oxygen, then dragged himself toward his wheelchair. He pulled it upright and set his sights on the slouching back of Thug 3. Ed's legs might be useless, but his arm strength was formidable. He launched the chair like a missile.

Strike! The chair hit its mark, and Thug 3 staggered forward. Ed briefly registered the look of surprise on Gaia's face as Thug 3 careened into her and sent her sprawling backward. His stomach clenched. Oh, God. That hadn't been his intention at all.

Now the guy retrieved his knife and leaped on top of Gaia. Worse yet, from Thug 2's cowardly hideout behind a parked car, he saw the tide turn and was racing back to join the fight. Ed dragged himself toward Gaia as fast as he could, his eyes fixed on her vulnerable throat and the knife hovering over it. "Stop!" he roared. "You're going to kill her!" He felt tears stinging his eyes.

It happened so fast, Ed wasn't sure he'd actually seen it. Gaia delivered a powerful kick exactly to the groin of Thug 2 and almost simultaneously struck Thug 3 in the side of the neck with her hand. Thug 3 rolled over, unconscious. His knife skidded along the stones. Thug 2 pitched to the ground, screaming in pain.

Gaia was instantly on her feet. She scooped up the knife and stepped over the prone body of Thug 3. Suddenly Thug 1 and Thug 2 seemed to forget their pain and sprinted for safety like jackrabbits in traffic.

Ed was watching Gaia, his heart overflowing with relief and admiration, when she surprised him again.

She got to the sidewalk and collapsed. Her legs literally crumpled under her body, and without a noise she fell in a heap on the pavement.

That Old Kryptonite

GAIA BREATHED DEEPLY AND WAITED for it to pass. She wouldn't struggle to move or attempt to get to her feet. She knew by now it wouldn't work. The only thing to do was wait.

Pretty much right on

schedule, she heard a noisy approach and felt a hand on her shoulder. Argh. She didn't need to open her eyes to see the worried, eager face.

Once he'd reached her, she heard him collapse beside her. Listening to his labored breathing, Gaia's heart was pulled forcefully by two equal and opposite desires:

1. Her desire to hug Ed for his valiant, misguided efforts on her behalf.
2. Her desire to murder him for being such an unbelievable pain in the ass.

"Are you okay?" He touched her shoulder again. She could hear the fear in his words.

She would have really liked to rouse herself right then. It was unthinkable that he should see her in `this state of weakness`—to see what happened to her after one of these episodes. And yet there was just no way around it short of killing him, which, though tempting, didn't seem all that sporting under the circumstances.

"Gaia? Gaia?" His voice was rising with panic.

"Mmmm," she mumbled.

"Oh, God, are you hurt? Did they hurt you?"

A yellow cab cruised past them, slowed for a stop sign, then drove on. If anyone in the car saw them, they apparently hadn't felt the need to get involved. That was New York City for you. Its inhabitants set a high standard for unusual.

With great effort she fluttered open her eyes and very slowly, by inches, shook her head. The sidewalk made a really bad pillow.

"What's the matter? Should I call for an ambulance?"

She gritted her teeth. If she'd had any energy left, she would have rolled her eyes. "Mm. Mmm." After another pause she reinforced it with another slight shake of her head.

"No? Are you sure?"

She wasn't accustomed to anyone seeing her like this, and it was irritating. She found the strength to open her eyes for real and concentrate on Ed's face. It had suddenly become a much more significant face—the face of the guy who knew her secrets.

Holy shit. How had she let this happen?

It was so ironic. So ironic and pitiful and stupid and weird, she wanted to laugh. For some reason this guy had become her self-appointed guardian angel and nearly gotten her killed in the process. How typical that her guardian angel would be a slightly scruffy ex-skate rat in a wheelchair who caused so much more trouble than good. How strange it was that he suddenly knew more about her than anyone else on planet Earth. (Except her father, of course.)

Gaia had been so careful over the years to keep

everything secret. It was another of her father's curses: *I'll make you into a freak and not let you tell anyone.* Not like she was going to tell, anyway. She had no confidant and meant to keep it that way. Besides, the strange facts of her life were all connected. Telling a little would ultimately mean telling a lot.

"Gaia? Please tell me you're okay?"

It always seemed that when her body sank into this state of paralytic exhaustion, her mind zoomed into overdrive. She summoned the energy to move her lips. "I'm fine," she whispered.

"You don't look so fine."

`Patience, Ed,` she asked of him silently. She felt the energy returning to her muscles. It was tingly at first, as if her whole body had fallen asleep. She groaned a little as she sat up. She studied Ed. Worried, terrified, astonished, concerned Ed. She couldn't help but smile a little.

"I'm fine," she said. She paused for breath. "Except for the fact that I may have to kill you."

To: L

From: ELJ

Date: September 25

File: 776244

Subject: Gaia Moore

Last Seen: Mercer Street, New York City, 10:53 P.M.

Update: Subject observed in fight with 3 suspected gang members, one armed with knife. Attack complicated by appearance of young man in wheelchair. Motive unclear. Confirmed subject's mastery of jujitsu. Subject displayed other martial skills previously documented. All 3 attackers subdued.

Subject appeared injured but later observed to walk from incident unharmed.

To: ELJ

From: L

Date: September 26

File: 776244

Subject: Gaia Moore

Directives: Identify and create file on young man in wheelchair.

Issue immediate instruction: Subject not to be injured under any circumstances. Repercussions will be severe.

GAIA

There is this other really freakish thing about me. I've never told anyone. I'd be way too humiliated.

Humiliation, by the way, is a truly terrible emotion. It's at the bottom of the pile. Much worse than fear, I bet. Since I don't have to have fear, why do I have to have humiliation? If only I could toss it wherever fear went. And while I was at it, I'd get rid of anger, hurt, compassion, betrayal. And selfishness. Oh, and guilt. Definitely guilt. It's out of there. Without all of those things, I think I could imagine maybe being happy someday.

Hey, that's it. I, Gaia Moore, have discovered the secret to happiness. People have been searching for it since the beginning of time, but it took me, a seventeen-year-old with no philosophical, medical, or psychological training, to discover the truth:

Lobotomy. You don't have to feel anything at all.

You heard it here first, folks. And a full frontal lobotomy probably costs no more than the average nose job.

Okay, where was I? Oh, yeah. No wonder I'm digressing—I don't feel like putting this into words.

I'm a virgin.

No, no. It's way worse than that. I wish it were only that.

I've never had a boyfriend.

True, but nope. That doesn't convey the depth of this particular humiliation.

I've never kissed anybody.

Okay, there you have it. Can you say "loser"?

Let me try to soften this information with an excuse or two. When I was twelve, I had something approaching a boyfriend, in a preboyfriend kind of way. His name was Stephen, and he lived around the corner. He was the one with the right kind of hair (light brown, straight, no cowlicks), the right kind of bike (specialized, like you care), the right kind of jeans (Gap, at the time). His parents had the right kind of car (red Jeep, good stereo) and a very large pool. For these reasons the popular girls sought him out. I liked him because he was secretly just as weird as me. We both played chess and knee football. We concocted these elaborate fantasy games set in Camelot or a mile under the sea, long after imaginary games are socially acceptable (age four, roughly). We were nerdy enough to watch Bill Nye, the Science Guy, but cool enough not to admit that to anybody but each other.

Hold on. Wait just a second. Why am I telling you all this? Am I really so desperate that I'll try to pass off a neighbor without underarm hair as some kind of romantic conquest? This represents a new low.

But it points to something

real, which is that I'm stunted. My love life got left behind with the rest of my life the autumn after my twelfth birthday. Eventually, when the moving van came, I told Stephen I hated him, just so as not to leave any threads dangling.

My life ended then, but I keep growing.

I usually pride myself on the fact that I don't care about being a freak or a misfit. I don't care what people think of me. But for some reason this kissing business, this lack of kissing business, bothers me, and I can't pretend it doesn't.

That's the very worst thing about it, really. How much it bothers me. How much I think about it.

I'm going to be brutally honest right now, and hopefully afterward I can snap back into some more comfortable state of denial.

Ready? Okay.

Of all the terrible things

that have happened in my life—my mom, my dad, the life I lost—I'm such a vain, petty, and selfish person that I am most ashamed of the fact that nobody has ever kissed me.

This thought drives me to more than the desire for a lobotomy. This drives me to something worse.

Yo, Rapunzel. Forget the ladder. There's a faster way down.

Ten years from now Heather's awfulness would have caught up with her, and she'd be a disgruntled wretch pining for the glory days.

bitch queen

"I STARTED THINKING/NOT DRINKING was better for me/so it got me to thinking/about getting a lobotomy . . ."

So Sweet, You'll Puke

"What did she just say?" Gaia was sitting behind a very large, very expensive mug of coffee across from Ed and squinting at the band that was playing in the far corner. Gaia was happy to ignore them. She'd seen plenty of unplugged garage bands in her day. But these weird snippets of songs kept floating into her consciousness and sticking there the way raspberry seeds stuck in her molars.

"Huh?" Ed asked.

"That singer. Did you hear the words?" Gaia asked.

Ed strained to listen over the clink of spoons and the hissing of the cappuccino machine. "Something about a lobotomy."

"You're joking," Gaia declared.

Ed gave her a puzzled look. "If so, it wasn't a very funny joke."

"No, I mean, she didn't actually say lobotomy."

"Okay, she didn't." Ed shrugged. "Why does it matter?"

Gaia stirred her coffee. "Never mind." She studied the singer. She looked a little like Ashley Judd before the makeup went on. An East Village version, anyway, with a wool stocking cap, hair so messy it was coagulating into dreads, and a tattoo of a spider that perched on her collarbone.

Gaia fidgeted in her chair. She didn't want to leave too much silence because Ed might bring up what happened last night and she really didn't want him to.

"You know what the problem is with these fancy brown sugar packets?" Gaia held one up. "The granules are too big. They don't dissolve. They just hang around in the bottom of your mug, so your coffee isn't as sweet as you want it to be until you get to the last sip, which is so sweet, you want to puke."

Ed looked both puzzled and slightly amused. "Huh. Hadn't thought of that." He gestured at the counter. "They have regular sugar up there."

Gaia nodded. Why had she gone for coffee after school with Ed?

Because he'd asked her, mainly. Because he'd tried to save her life, even though she'd ended up saving his. She should have remembered, before she'd accepted, that going for coffee with someone usually meant talking to them.

Ed was looking at her a little too meaningfully. He stretched his arms out in front of him. "Listen, Gaia, I just wanted to tell you that I—"

"I don't want to talk about it," Gaia jumped in quickly.

"Sorry?"

"I don't want to talk about it."

"What is *it?*"

Now he really was going to think she was a wacko. "It. Anything."

"You don't want to talk about anything?" Ed asked carefully.

Gaia tugged at her hair awkwardly. "I don't want to talk about last night. I don't want you to ask me any questions."

Ed nodded and digested that for a minute. "Hey, Gaia?"

"Yeah."

"I'll make you a promise."

"That sounds heavy."

Ed laughed. "Just listen, okay?"

"Okay."

"I promise that I won't ever ask you any questions, all right?"

Gaia laughed, too. "I think that was a question."

"Fine, so it was the last one."

"Fine."

Gaia was starting to sense `too much friendliness in the air`, so she stood up. "I'm going to, um, get that regular sugar. I'll be right back."

"Good."

"Okay."

She walked to the counter with her mug. This

was so cozy and normal seeming, she felt as if she were inhabiting somebody else's body. Absently she dumped two packets of white sugar into her coffee.

Oh, yes, she was just a happy girl in the West Village, having coffee with a friend.

A troop of familiar-looking people streamed in. They were from school, she realized. The self-designated "beautiful people." There were three girls and two guys, and they were laughing about something. Their manner and wardrobe screamed, "Put me in a Banana Republic ad right now!" One girl in particular was quite beautiful, with long, shiny dark hair, slouchy chinos, and a collared shirt that was whiter and crisper than anything Gaia had ever owned.

Much as she wanted to dismiss them as they swarmed around her at the counter, ordering various combinations of lattes, au laits, con leches, and mochas in pretentious Italian sizes, Gaia couldn't help imagining some alternate universe where she was one of them.

What if she were witty and well dressed and carefree? What if her biggest dilemma in life were whether to order a grande latte or a magnifico mocha? What if that fairly cute one, the boy in the beat-up suede jacket, called her all the time? She studied his dark hair, so pleasantly dilapidated, and his hazel eyes. She allowed herself a look at his lips. What if he'd kissed her? Not just once but hundreds of times?

She felt a weird tingling in her lower extremities as the fantasy evolved in her mind. He'd be standing next to her, studying the coffee board, as familiar to her as a brother, and he'd reach for her without really thinking about it. She'd be wearing a cute little lavender sweater set and crisp khakis instead of these oversized drawstring army pants and her faded blue football tee. He'd loop an arm around her hips and draw her a little closer and order something she knew he'd order because he always ordered it. Then he'd order for her, too. Not because he was an asinine pig, but because he knew she loved hazelnut mochaccino even though it did cost six dollars. Then he'd pay, even though she'd tell him not to. And she'd say something so funny and adorable that he'd look at her, really look at her, and remember how beautiful she was and how much he loved her. Then he'd lean toward her and kiss her on the mouth. No tongue or anything. That would be tacky in the middle of a cafe. His kiss wouldn't be long or filled with questions or expectations because he could kiss her anytime he wanted and he didn't have anything to prove. It would be soft and real and simple, yet mean a thousand loving things. She would kiss him back, but not in a way that was desperate or inexperienced. And then—

Gaia suddenly realized that the boy she was kissing in her mind's eye had transformed. Gone were the dark hair and the suede jacket, replaced by ginger-colored hair that curled around his temples and a preppy gray twill jacket with a corduroy collar. And then she realized that this person who'd barged right into her fantasy was none other than him, the guy from the park—the guy who'd wandered by the chess tables. How did he get here? she demanded of herself stridently. Who invited *him?*

"Gaia?"

She was so startled and unnerved that she forgot she even had hands, let alone a steaming mug of coffee in one of them. In horror she watched the mug sail from her grasp and the brown sugary stuff leap out of it and land all over the front of that very white, very crisp shirt of her alternate-universe best girlfriend.

The girl screamed.

"Oh, shit," Gaia muttered.

Suddenly everybody burst into motion: The fairly cute boy was grabbing up napkins, the girls were buzzing all over their friend, the other boy was plucking pieces of mug from the mess on the floor.

Of course, Gaia knew that the right thing to do was

apologize a lot, hand the girl a few napkins, make a self-deprecating remark, and offer to get her shirt dry cleaned. But for some reason Gaia did none of those things. She just stood there, gaping like a complete moron.

The offended girl turned on her with narrowed eyes. "*Excuse* me, but you just poured boiling coffee down my shirt."

"I—," Gaia began.

"What the hell is your problem? Are you some kind of idiot? Could you at least apologize?" The girl didn't look so pretty anymore.

"I just—I—I'm really—"

"Hel-*lo?*" the girl demanded. "English? Do you speak English? *Habla español?*" This was apparently humorous to herself and to her friends.

Gaia really had been working up to a sincere and heartfelt apology, but this girl no longer deserved it. "Bitch," Gaia said under her breath. It was completely the wrong thing to do. The worst thing to do, but Gaia had a talent for that.

The ex–pretty girl stiffened. "*What?* Did you just say what I think you said? Who the hell do you think you are?"

Gaia turned away at this point. It was the only thing to do. Gaia heard the girl railing and threatening as she returned to the table and a shell-shocked-looking Ed.

"Gaia, can I ask you one question, just one, and this is really the last?" Ed didn't wait for her to respond.

"Do you get in fights *everywhere* you go?"

"MARCO! OVER HERE."

There's This Girl

Marco glanced around the Chinese restaurant casually, as if he hadn't noticed her the instant he'd walked through the door. Man, she was hot. She was wearing dark denim jeans today and a formfitting pink sweater.

"Hey, how's it going?" he said, treating her to his most charming smile and sitting down across from her.

She returned his smile and for a moment laid her hand on top of his. She was making him dizzy again.

A waiter hustled by and dropped two menus. The place was still noisy, but the after-school crowds were clearing out. Marco checked his hair quickly in the mirror that coated the restaurant's side wall. He was glad he'd refused to shave his head like the other guys. He consulted the filthy laminated menu. Was he supposed to order something? He suspected she hadn't asked him to meet her here because she was hungry.

"So, Marco, tell me how you've been." She was studying him intently and ignoring her menu. She leaned close. He felt a gentle foot on his.

Yes, dizzy. *Really dizzy.* "I've been, uh, pretty cool." He swallowed.

"What's been going on in the park?"

Shit. Was he supposed to be able to think when she was doing that with her foot?

"Not much," he said. "Couple of my buddies got beat up last night."

She looked more interested than concerned. "Who did it?"

"I'm not sure. Some real tough guys, I guess. Some guys who know how to fight." Now her foot was gone, and *he really wanted it back.*

"You'll get them," she said confidently.

He liked the way she said it and the way she looked at him. He nodded real slow, the way his buddy Martin's older brother did. "Bet your ass," he said.

"I need to ask you something," she said.

Where was her foot? Had he done something wrong? "Yeah?"

"There's this girl, a friend of mine. She likes to hang out in the park. I know there's a lot of stuff going on. You know, slashing and whatever."

"I heard about that," he said, his look just as knowing as hers.

"I want to make sure nobody touches her, okay? She's a real sweetheart, and I don't want her getting hurt."

The foot was back. Marco felt a dull buzz in his ears. "Right. Okay. You point her out to me in the park, and I'll take care of it."

The restaurant was nearly empty now. The waiters were sitting at a round table at the very back, eating their own snack. Marco felt a hand on his knee under the table. He had to stifle a groan. He leaned toward her and snaked his hand around the back of her neck. He kissed her hard, and she kissed him back. Her sweet smell combined with the heavy scents of fried wontons and cabbage. Her soft, blissful tongue explored his while the brown Formica table jammed into his stomach. God, he wanted to do it right here.

Suddenly her tongue and her hands were gone and she was standing. "Come on." She gestured at the door. "I know a place we can go."

ED SAW HER THE FOLLOWING AFTERnoon, sitting at a chess table near the southwestern corner of the park, and his heart sped up a little. The late September breeze was blowing her blond hair out of its messy ponytail and around her face. She'd shed her rumpled jacket to reveal a sleeveless white T-shirt and lithe, sculpted shoulders. Her muscles were defined, but long and graceful. In the sunshine he noticed a few freckles along the bridge of her nose. Her eyes looked less stormy gray and more Caribbean turquoise in this light.

Her opponent at the chessboard was a man in his thirties wearing a baseball cap and a pair of expensive sneakers and appearing to concentrate about ten times harder than she was.

She was wearing an expression he hadn't seen on her before—sort of wide-eyed and distracted. She gazed around. She examined her fingernails. She even appeared to giggle while losing a pawn. Was this actually Gaia?

Ed's legs were for crap, but his eyes were excellent. It was definitely Gaia. Either that or her ditzy twin sister.

He watched in surprise as she lost two more pawns and a knight. Her opponent was looking pretty pleased with himself. He was also allowing his eyes a few breaks from the board to gawk at Gaia. *Pervert,* Ed thought irritably.

Gaia lost another pawn. She might be able to take Bruce Lee in a fight, but she sure sucked at chess. She giggled again. It was a weird sound. Like a parakeet mooing or something. What was up with her?

Gaia's opponent snatched up her rook, and suddenly her manner changed. She focused with a slight frown on the board and started making moves rapidly. The man was smiling at her when she looked up from the board again. He looked so patronizing and full of himself that Ed suspected he was about to ask her out. He hoped Gaia would break his jaw.

Instead she said, "Checkmate," in a matter-of-fact way. Ed read her lips more than actually heard her say it.

Ed watched with blossoming pleasure as the man's face fell and his mouth snapped shut. He looked confused, then a bit suspicious, and then downright sour as he pulled out his wallet and handed over a twenty. As he walked away with his *New York Times* tucked under his arm, his overly youthful baseball cap looked even more absurd. Maybe he was in his forties.

"Go, Gaia," Ed said, wheeling over.

She turned toward his voice, her eyebrows connecting over angry eyes. "What, are you spying on me?"

"No, I'm strolling through the park and stopping to say hi to a friend," he countered. "A paranoid friend." He *was* basically spying, but she didn't need to know that.

Her fierce eyes relented a bit. "Oh."

"I see you discovered how to play chess right there in the middle of the game. Wow."

She cocked her head and almost smiled. "Gee, yeah. Lucky timing, huh?"

"And you made twenty dollars to boot," Ed added.

"Poor bastard didn't know what hit him."

"So you were spying," Gaia accused, but she didn't look mad anymore.

"Maybe a little," he admitted.

She sighed. "You know, Ed, if you learn any more of my secrets, I really will have to kill you." She stood and slung her weather-beaten messenger bag over her shoulder.

He shrugged. "Okay. I guess."

She started walking toward Washington Place, and he followed her.

"But before you do," he continued, "I was wondering, will you go to a party with me tonight?"

She stopped and turned on him, her eyebrows drawing together again. "Are you joking? Of course not."

Since his accident Ed had become a near professional button pusher, but nobody's buttons gave him quite the thrill that Gaia's did. Most people pretended to be civil for far too long. Gaia got spitting mad right away.

"Come on, it's a school party. Allison Rovitz is having it—you know, Heather's friend?"

"Who's Heather?" She was walking again.

"The girl you, uh, met over coffee yesterday," Ed said, quickly catching up with her.

Gaia shook her head in disbelief. "Boy, you sure do make it sound tempting."

Ed nodded. "It might be fun. Besides, it would be

good for you to meet some people," he suggested brightly.

Gaia stopped short and glanced around her. "What is going on here? Are the cameras rolling? Are we secretly starring in an after-school special? *Wheelchair Boy Befriends Angry Orphan Girl*?"

Ed laughed genuinely. "So I'll meet you there at nine? I'll leave the address on your answering machine."

"No!" Gaia almost shouted.

"Why not?" Ed persisted. "You don't have anything else to do."

"Yes, I do," she shot back.

"Like what?" Ed demanded.

She was silent for a few seconds. "Okay, I don't." Gaia glared at him. "Rub it in."

Ed loved the way she pressed her lips together. He loved the way she stood with one hip stuck out. He tried not to be obvious when he admired the way her hair fell perfectly, framing her face and stunning eyes, no matter how hard the wind tore at it. He had heard of this mythic species, beautiful girls who were not conscious of the fact that they were beautiful. He'd seen them represented in movies and on TV—unconvincingly for the most part. He'd read about them in books. But he'd never actually met one in person until Gaia.

"I know why you won't go," Ed said suddenly.

Gaia's patience was waning. "Why?"

"Because Heather's going to be there. You're scared of Heather," Ed stated confidently.

Gaia put her hands on her hips. She looked like she really did want to kill him. "Ed. I am not *scared* of Heather. Trust me."

Klutz Girl Strikes Again

WHAT IN THE WORLD WAS SHE doing? Gaia walked extra fast along Seventh Avenue, past Bleecker, past the duplex psychic shop blazing with neon, past the shop (one of many) that pierced you anyplace you could think of, past the bustling gay bars on Christopher Street.

As much as she despised getting railroaded into a stupid party full of people she was sure to hate, there was a small but unsquashable part of her that was happy to be out on a Saturday night with someplace to go.

She was going because she wasn't afraid of Heather and because she really didn't have anything else to do.

But she was mostly going because Ed had asked her. He was the first person in her entire high school career who'd cut through her defenses long enough to ask her to a party. He was the first person she hadn't succeeded in scaring off, in spite of her usual efforts.

The party was at 25 West Fifteenth Street. West meant west of Fifth Avenue, but not by much, so she hung a right at Fifteenth. Weeks ago, before she'd even moved here, she had committed a map of lower Manhattan to her near perfect visual memory.

She glanced down at her dark jeans and trashed sneakers. It would be impossible to tell from looking at her that she had spent over an hour getting dressed. She'd put on some mascara, then washed it off. She'd tried on three pairs of nearly identical jeans before finally closing her eyes and grabbing a pair randomly. She'd even changed her socks. Her one lasting concession to beauty was buried under shoes and (carefully chosen) socks—toenail polish in a hue called Cockroach.

As the address grew near, she spied one of the things she most disliked about New York residential life: a doorman. How much did you have to pay a guy to dress up in a butt-ugly polyester suit and embarrassing hat and open your damn door? And where were the door*women*, anyway? She hadn't seen a single one since she'd been here. Maybe she'd change her life's ambition from waitress to doorwoman. "Doorwoman." It sounded like some postmodern urban superhero.

Of course, this particular doorman wanted to know her name and whose apartment she felt privileged enough to visit. "Ed Fargo," she told him. "Visiting Allison Rovitz in apartment 12C."

The doorfellow gave her a once-over. "You don't look like an Ed."

"Tell my parents that. It's a real burden," she told him.

He shook his head, as though wishing he never had to speak to another scruffy, attitude-wielding seventeen-year-old as long as he lived.

He consulted his list, then waved a hand toward the inner lobby. "Go ahead."

"Why aren't there any doorwomen?" she nearly shouted after him as the elevator door closed.

The party in 12C could be heard throughout 12, from what Gaia could tell. She felt her muscles tense at the shrieks of laughter and loud buzz of conversation spilling into the hallway. `This was kind of a momentous event.` Although her capacity for nervousness was nil, her capacity for insecurity was all there. She tucked some hair behind her ear. She took a deep breath and pushed open the unlocked door.

What was she expecting exactly? Some deeply

narcissistic part of her thought everybody in the place would know that even though she was a junior, she had never been to a real high school party before. They would fall silent and turn to stare at her.

In fact, the only difference between before she had come and after was that there was one more beating heart in a very crowded apartment.

Okeydoke. Yes, here she was. Suddenly she was sure she'd been born with an extra gene for social awkwardness. Time to find the real Ed Fargo and hope he still thought she was entertaining.

She squeezed past a knot of people in the foyer who didn't care about her at all. In the living room she recognized a girl from her history class, a couple of guys who had lockers near hers. Every flat surface was covered with soda cans and beer cans in about equal number. A lot of people were smoking—mostly girls. On a table in the corner were raw carrots and dip and some unappealing chips and salsa. The meager food table was quickly being taken over by cans and cans and cans and makeshift ashtrays. Were anybody's parents here? She'd heard that New York City parents let their kids drink at parties because nobody drove anywhere afterward.

The sweet, suffocating smell of marijuana made its way over. She zeroed in on the little clutch of people passing around the joint before she turned and walked in the opposite direction. She had less than no time for that. Were those kids really so confident in their sanity, they could tempt fate?

When she finally caught sight of Ed's wheelchair in the dining room, she stifled the strong urge to sprint over to him and give him a hug. She walked toward him as slowly as she could manage, as though expecting to encounter hordes of friends and acquaintances along the way.

Gaia was shy. She'd forgotten that about herself, but she was. She was more comfortable beating the crap out of somebody than chatting about the weather. She could be sullen and obnoxious and irritable all day long, but she couldn't think of a single way to start a friendly conversation.

"Hi, Ed," she said lamely, once she was near.

"Gaia! Holy shit!" He smiled big. "You actually came."

"I never miss a party," she said wryly.

"Wow. You look great," he said.

"No, I don't."

"Okay, you don't. Hey, this is Claire." He pointed at a long-haired Asian girl he'd been talking to. "Claire, this is Gaia."

Claire waved and smiled. She was smoking a cigarette.

"And this is Mary. Mary, Gaia, et cetera."

Mary was tall, with wavy red hair. She waved in a

perfunctory way and took a swig of beer.

"You're new, right?" Claire asked.

"Yes," Gaia answered.

"Where are you from?" Claire wanted to know.

Ed shifted in his chair.

Gaia cleared her throat. "Uh. Memphis." It was a lie. She didn't want to play the "oh, really, do you know . . . ?" game about anyplace she had actually lived.

"Really? I have a cousin in Tennessee," Claire responded predictably. "In Johnson City."

"Oh?" Gaia nodded blankly.

Suddenly there was a swell of noise from the direction of the front door. All eyes turned.

"Hey, Gaia, check it out," Ed said. "It's your best friend."

Gaia gave him a mean look. It was Heather and friends—the same group from the cafe plus a couple of Hollywood extras. Heather really was beautiful when she wasn't snarling. Judging from the energy she and her crowd brought into the apartment with them, the party had only started at that moment.

Claire studied the group carefully. "I guess Heather didn't bring her boyfriend. Too bad. That guy is altogether hot."

Mary looked unimpressed. "He's a big college man. He goes to NYU. What's his name again? Carrie says he doesn't like coming to high school parties."

Of course Heather would have a gorgeous, snotty boyfriend who was in college. Of course. Gaia could only imagine what kind of asshole the guy must be to choose Heather as a girlfriend.

"I guess we're blessed even to have Heather," Gaia mumbled, instantly cursing herself for being snide.

Mary glanced at Gaia appreciatively. "Yes. I mean, who better to make the rest of us feel fat and friendless?"

Gaia laughed and felt a surge of . . . something. Optimism, was it? Hope? Social acceptance? She wasn't sure exactly—it was so unfamiliar. But here she was, maladjusted freak-thing Gaia Moore, gabbing with people who could very easily have been her friends. It was utterly alien, but not in a bad way. Only now she had to try to think of something else to say.

Heather led the wave of party energy through the living room toward the dining room and, no doubt, the kitchen, where the beers were waiting. Gaia wondered a bit warily if Heather would recognize her.

As it turned out, she did.

"Oh, my God!" Heather shrieked, wheeling around to face Gaia straight on. "It's Klutz Girl! What are you doing here?"

Suddenly all eyes really were on Gaia. Her social success was evaporating quickly.

"I would watch out for this girl," Heather warned loudly. "Don't give her anything to eat or drink, or you'll end up with it on your shirt."

Heather's friends tittered loyally.

"Who let you in here?" Heather demanded.

Gaia studied the small place on the girl's neck just below her chin. She could deliver one swift blow to that spot and put her out.

"I invited her," Ed said, filling the awkward silence at least momentarily.

"Excuse me, *Ed*," Heather said nastily. "I didn't realize it was your party."

"I didn't realize it was yours," Ed responded.

Allison, the actual party giver, was watching the scene unfold with the rest of them. Heather turned to her.

"Al, did you realize this bitch was coming to your party?"

Poor Allison looked frightened.

"Don't worry about it, Allison. I'm going," Gaia said. She strode through the apartment without looking back.

It didn't matter so much that she was back on the outside, Gaia consoled herself as she opened the front door and passed through it. This was Heather's time. Let her have it. Ten years from now Heather's awfulness would have caught up with her, and she'd be a disgruntled wretch pining for the glory days. Let her have high school. Gaia was holding out for something better.

Gaia stood sullenly at the elevator bank and punched the down arrow. Mercifully the elevator doors opened right away.

At least she was back in her comfort zone.

Some things I like:
Chess
Slurpees
Road Runner cartoons
Eye boogers
W. B. Yeats
Ed

Some things I don't like:
Heather
Ella
Skim milk
Butterflies
Baking soda toothpaste
Myself

A thing I hate:
My dad

Rain plastered
thick dark
cords of hair
to his fore-
head.

Now that it
was no longer
perfect,
she could see
it was
beautiful.

meeting sam moon

"HI, ZOLOV."

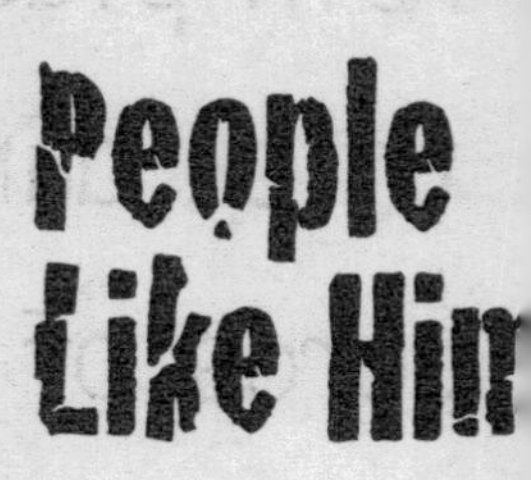

The old man squinted at Gaia for a few seconds before he recognized her, then he smiled.

"Hey, Curtis," she said to Zolov's opponent. "Where's Renny?"

The fifteen-year-old chess fixture shrugged. "He hasn't been coming around anymore."

Gaia nodded and looked for a free table. She was happy to be there, even without Renny. She was glad that the bleak sky threatened rain and that the air was finally turning cold. All that warm sunshine seemed to demand perkiness and pastel-colored clothing.

She watched Curtis leaning far over the board, studying Zolov's sequence. She almost laughed to herself. She couldn't believe she was watching an ancient Jewish man in a threadbare wool overcoat teaching the Ruy Lopez opening to a black kid dressed head to toe in Tommy.

She turned her affectionate gaze to the right, and suddenly her mood went into free fall.

Him.

What the hell was *he* doing here?

God, he was good-looking. He was wearing that same gray jacket, this time with a pair of jeans and just the right shade of dark, perfectly scuffed leather shoes.

Go away, she ordered him silently. Go back to where you belong.

He didn't go away. Instead he came very close, and her mouth felt dry. Why did she all of a sudden care that she hadn't run a brush through her hair that morning? So she looked like a homeless person. What was it to him?

Oh, shit. He was looking at the board set in front of her. His eyes glanced over the empty chair across from her.

He was stopping!

He was sitting down!

He was staring right at her!

Then she felt mad. What, was he on some kind of field trip from normal-people land? Was he the Jane Goodall of the popular set, here to take notes?

It didn't help that just a few days before he'd appeared *uninvited* in her romantic fantasy and *kissed* her, for God's sake. "Do you want to play?" he asked, just like that.

He wanted to play her! What! Didn't he know that it was illegal in a cosmic sense for a guy who looked like him even to get near a board? The gods of social stratification would zap him but good.

Fine. If he insisted on turning the world upside down, what could she do? She'd play him. She'd point out to him which pieces moved which way as though she'd only recently learned herself, and then she'd hustle as much money out of him as possible. She could probably get two or three fast games out of him before the rain began to fall.

"Hello?" He scrunched down a little in his chair to try to gain eye contact.

"What?" she blurted out irritably.

"Do you want to play?"

She was so flustered, she couldn't pluck one arrow from her quiver of hustling tricks. "Fine."

"Don't feel like you have to."

Oh, wasn't he just honorable.

"No, it's fine. I only just started playing myself." God, she sounded wooden. Her acting really needed some work.

"Okay. You start, right?"

"No, I mean, I think. Well, we usually—" Dammit. She took a black pawn and a white one and mixed them up behind her back. She enclosed each in a fist and stuck them out toward him. "You pick."

He pointed to her left hand, and she produced a white pawn.

"You go first," she said.

He looked tentative. "It's kind of a custom to play for money here, isn't it?"

Custom? Yes, it is, O Great Doctor of Losers.

"Usually," was what she said.

"How much?"

"I dunno. Twenty?"

He blew out his breath. "Wow. Okay."

"Okay."

What was it about him that bothered her so? That he was the kind of guy who'd never look twice at a girl like her? Okay, well, there was that.

She couldn't find major fault with his wardrobe. It wasn't like he was wearing a Rolex or anything.

She didn't hate him just because he looked like . . . that. Even she wasn't quite that shallow or rabidly judgmental.

What was it, then?

He was so . . . confident. That was the big problem. Here, in her place, where he had no right to be, he was so goddamned sure of himself. He probably had no sense of humor, least of all about himself.

She couldn't wait to kick his ass.

The Fire Hose Test

SAM MOON WASN'T SURE WHAT TO make of this girl. He'd sat down at her board because she was new, and that always represented an opportunity.

Well, okay. That wasn't the only reason. Another reason

was that in spite of her somewhat disastrous personal hygiene, she was pretty. A pretty girl at a chessboard wasn't your everyday sight. He hadn't even realized just how pretty until he was within a couple of feet and had a chance to really look.

Some friends of his from high school used to rate a girl's attractiveness by what was known as `the fire hose test.` If the girl's looks were all about makeup and hair and clothes, she'd look like crap if you shot a fire hose directly in her face from point-blank range. A genuinely pretty girl would still look good. Now, this girl here looked as though a hose actually had blasted her, so `there was no leap of imagination necessary to know that she passed the test.` Passed it with an A, he decided as she bit her lip and tapped impatiently on the queen's pawn.

"Okay, here goes," he said, thumping to E4.

She predictably took E5.

Pretty as she was, though, she was annoying. She obviously thought she knew what she was doing—under her truly flimsy pretense that she didn't. Maybe she'd won some high school tournament or something. Whoop-de-do. She had no business taking over a table here.

And why was she glaring at him like that? What had he done to piss her off?

`He'd give her hope for a few`

minutes and then shut her down. He could really use the twenty bucks.

He flinched a little as a clap of thunder roared overhead. The air felt heavy with coming rain. He'd give her a very few minutes.

The Rain Starts

SHE WAS SURPRISED. NOT ALARMED or anything. Just a little surprised.

She hadn't expected him to respond so adroitly to her opening. They'd progressed quickly to the midgame, and she'd achieved almost no advantage. Now the wind was blowing in soot-colored clouds and thunder rolled through the sky and she was looking at the possibility of a complicated endgame.

He wasn't the doofus she'd imagined. That much she had to admit. She hadn't thought it possible to have perfect orthodonture and a good haircut and also be great at chess, but then, she was only seventeen. There had to be a few things left to learn.

She wasn't pretending anything anymore. She was too focused on the board. All attempts at inane, gee-whiz posturing had fallen away.

His manner had changed, too. His concentration on the game was so full, he let out these tiny, almost inaudible grunts every so often. He had this funny tick of drumming his fingers against his bottom lip before he made each move. She couldn't exactly remember what about him had seemed so self-satisfied.

She unintentionally knocked her knee against his under the table. He glanced up.

"Sorry," she mumbled. Her face felt warm. She prayed it wasn't actually turning pink.

His hair had fallen over his forehead. She couldn't read the expression in his eyes.

She commanded her own eyeballs back to the board.

A fat, cold raindrop landed on her scalp. Damn. Why couldn't she just finish this up?

More Rain

TINY DROPS OF SWEAT WERE collecting in his hairline, bleeding into the raindrops slapping on his head. Drops dribbled down his neck, and his sweater was starting to smell funky. He was concentrating too hard to care.

The girl moved her king's bishop.

Ugh. He closed his eyes briefly in disgust at himself. Why hadn't he seen the pin? What was wrong with him?

He was forced to defend with a knight. That was a tempo lost.

The main thing wrong was that this girl was totally shocking. She was not good. She was very, very, very good. Where had she come from? She couldn't be from around here because he felt sure he would have met her in tournaments before. She had to be an internationally ranked player. Either that or he suddenly stunk.

He'd sacrificed material to no avail. She'd dismantled one of his most trusted combinations. But even so, it was a really exciting game. Her play was not only smart and challenging, but unorthodox. Who had taught her? Who was she?

He glanced up at her. Her light hair was soaked flat with rain. Her blue eyes darkened to mirror the sky, and they were steady with concentration. She was somewhere around sixteen or seventeen years old. He hadn't detected any accent, which would have at least helped to explain how she was so good. It seemed like foreign players always dominated in competition.

The harsh, defiant set of her face had dissolved now. Self-consciousness had fallen away as her focus intensified. Her eyes were lovely, rimmed with long, dark (wet) lashes. Her cheekbones were exceptionally prominent for a person her age. Her face was open now and almost sweet. Raindrops stood on her bare arms, and her T-shirt was . . .

She snapped her rook into the center of the action.

Okay, better not to look anymore. He was screwing up here. Lucky for him there weren't many beautiful girls who played chess, or he'd probably be bowling right now.

His heart was speeding with nervousness and excitement. He could feel warmth radiating from her legs, so close to his. His palms felt tingly.

Think about chess, you idiot, he ordered himself.

A Flood

YES, ALARMING. IT WAS NOW officially alarming. He was up a knight and coming on strong. How had she misjudged him so badly?

He was probably the best person she had ever played except for her father, maybe, and Zolov, who was nuts.

She studied his face. He was older than she, but not by much. Maybe twenty. He had to be an international master at least. She wasn't on the chess circuit, but she knew an extraordinary player from a good one.

And as he played he was becoming real to her. His

little ticks were so peculiar. The skin around his fingernails was ragged from being picked at too much. Tiny blue veins zigzagged under the surface of the transparent skin beneath his eyes. Rain plastered thick dark cords of hair to his forehead. Now that it was no longer perfect, she could see it was beautiful.

Suddenly she had this powerful urge to touch the pale skin above his wrist, where she could see his pulse thumping. She stared transfixed at that spot, feeling that her own heart was beating out the same rhythm.

Oh, Gaia. She almost groaned out loud. Get ahold of yourself, girl.

This was an inexplicable reaction she was having to him. Was she profoundly low on sleep, maybe? When had she last eaten?

Another bolt of lightning blazed through the sky. Maybe it was the plunging barometer? The electricity in the air?

When she looked back at the board, she felt dizzy and disoriented. A chess game like this one meant holding a million teetering moves and possibilities in your mind, and here all at once she'd dropped them. The crowd of pieces left on the board had gone from a thrillingly complex and significant battle in one second to a meaningless jumble the next.

Blood rushed to her face. She tried to kick-start her

memory, to patch together her lost strategy. But it was as though the whole thing had existed in someone else's mind.

Rain blanketed them. Steam rose from the surrounding pavement. Goose bumps pricked up and down her arms. Why had neither of them suggested giving up this ridiculous contest and going inside?

He was looking at her. Not silently, impatiently demanding her next move, as she would expect. Just looking. Looking for something. Rain dotted his eyelashes with diamonds, formed rivers down his cheeks.

His eyes had taken hers, and she couldn't look away.

Then she felt something grab hold of her chest. It wasn't fear. It couldn't be. But what was it? She had to get out of there.

With a flick of her index finger she felled her precious king. "I'm sorry," she murmured. "I have to go." She got to her feet, reaching into her bag for her wallet. He stood, too. She fumbled the wet leather and pulled out a twenty-dollar bill, then jammed it in his palm.

"No. No," he told her. The bill fluttered to the ground, but neither of them stooped to get it. She was already walking, and he was hurrying alongside her, confused, surprised, stammering for a word.

"W-Wait. Please," he whispered.

She was almost running. In her sneakers the water squished around her toes. The rain was so loud, it filled up all of her senses.

She hurried from him and from the strange perception that a million frozen feelings were about to thaw and the flood would certainly drown her.

HE WATCHED HER GO, FEELING A

Bottomless

terrible tightness in his throat. What had she done to him?

It had all happened in that moment, when he'd met her eyes and, like a mystic, seemed to see her past and future. Her past was haunting, marked by bottomless wounds, and the future was terrifying because it included him.

For the last
twenty-four
hours his
mind had
behaved
more like a
badly
trained
dog on a
too long
leash.

no
bad
dogs

"I WISH MY NAME WERE FARGO."

The Right to Ask

Gaia was walking so fast, Ed Fargo was having a hard time keeping up with her. Her movements were strangely jerky, and her mouth was going a mile a minute.

"Why is that?" he had to practically shout at her because she kept getting ahead.

"It's a cool name," she said.

"You could marry me if you asked really nicely," he proposed.

"Yeah, right."

"What's the matter with Moore?" he asked as they rounded the corner of Charles Street and Hudson.

"I don't know." Gaia's eyes weren't quite focused. She wasn't completely paying attention to what she was saying or where her feet were going. "Moore . . . Less," she mused absently. "Hey, Gaia Less. Guileless. I like that."

He was getting annoyed. "Gaia, would you please slow down? I'm kind of in a wheelchair here."

She glanced back at him. "Oh. Sorry," she mumbled.

In her expression Ed saw traces of impatience but no embarrassment, no pity. He loved her.

"Guileless," he continued. "What does it mean?"

"You know, without guile."

"What does guile mean?"

"Deceit, duplicity, dishonesty."

He slowed down a bit more. "Gaia, how do you know these things?"

She shrugged. "I'm smart."

"And modest, too."

"Modesty is a waste of time," she pronounced.

"I'll keep that in mind."

They passed Zuli's bakery and the tiny store that sold homemade ravioli. A woman passed them, pushing a toy poodle perched in a baby carriage. Gaia didn't even seem to notice.

"For somebody so smart, you sure bombed the physics quiz today," Ed pointed out.

"Yeah, well. Parabolas are so simple, they're boring."

Ed laughed. "I'll have to remember that excuse to tell my parents the next time I get a D."

Suddenly Gaia stopped and grabbed his shoulder. "What's that?"

"Ouch," he said, and she lessened her grip on his clavicle. "What?"

"That music." She yanked him around the corner. "Do you hear it? Where's it coming from?"

He pointed across the street. "That band we heard at Ozzie's. They practice in the basement of that building."

"How do you know?"

"Because I'm smart."

Gaia rolled her eyes. "What's the name of the band?"

"Huh?"

"The name of the band?"

"Fearless. They're always playing around the neighborhood. Ozzie's on Friday afternoons, Dock's on Wednesday evenings, and fully amplified at The Flood most Saturday nights. Our local OTB takes bets on when they'll actually get signed."

Gaia had completely tuned out.

"Ha-ha. That was a funny joke," Ed pointed out.

Gaia nodded dumbly. "Fearless?" she asked. "No way."

Ed shrugged. "No reason to lie." He was bored with this conversation.

Gaia paused for another moment as slow lyrics drifted up to the street.

". . . And I'm a stone/falling deeper/into your black, black ocean/let me drown . . ."

Gaia was off again like a shot.

"Where are we going now?" he asked, almost breathless in his effort to catch up.

"I don't know. We're strolling."

"Oh."

They strolled for a while in silence.

"Hey, wait a minute," he said, slowing down warily as they sailed past Sixth Avenue without a pause.

"What?"

"I have a feeling we're strolling to the park."

"So?"

"I don't want to go to the park."

Gaia looked annoyed. "Why not?"

"Because innocent people are getting slashed there practically every day. Because there are evil bald guys carving swastikas into trees. Do you watch the news?"

"Ed, it's broad daylight."

"That doesn't stop you."

"Stop *me?* Stop me from what?" she asked.

"From finding people to get into fights with," he responded.

She looked slightly abashed.

"Let's walk down Broadway toward Soho," he suggested.

Gaia was quiet, fidgeting with the threads hanging off the bottom of her jacket, but she did follow him at least.

"What's the matter?" he asked.

"I'm trying to think of a way to apologize for the other night," she explained.

"What do you mean?" he asked.

"For ruining that party you invited me to."

"You didn't ruin it," he said comfortingly. "We all had a perfectly good time after you left."

She kicked his wheel.

"Gaia, Jesus!" He regained control of his chair. "I was just kidding. I left right away. I tried to catch you, but you were too fast for me."

She slowed down a little. "Really?"

"Yeah. Anyway, it wasn't you. It was Heather who was out of control."

"You think so?"

He laughed. "For once, yeah."

"She's such a raving bitch," Gaia declared.

Ed shook his head thoughtfully. "There's actually more to her than that."

"You know her well?" Gaia asked, clearly surprised.

"Sure. I went out with her for a few months."

Gaia stopped cold in the middle of Bleecker Street. A truck honked loudly.

"Gaia, go!" Ed commanded, and she did.

"No way," she stated when they were safely on the other side of the street.

Ed looked at her peevishly. "You say that too much."

"Sorry. But I mean it. No way."

Ed held up his hands. "It's true. Heather and I went out for a while before my accident."

"Wow." Gaia was obviously struggling to absorb this. They walked for three blocks in silence.

"Hey, Gaia?" he asked finally.

"Yeah?"

"Are you ever going to ask me why I'm in a wheelchair?"

"No," she said.

"Why not?"

"Because if I do, you would have the right to ask

where I lived before, or why I'm a black belt in karate, or what happened to my parents."

"Oh," he said. "Okay."

And they kept walking.

That Girl

SAM WASN'T WALKING THROUGH THE park because he wanted to see that girl. He didn't want to see that girl. She was trouble.

And he had a girlfriend. That was the more important point. He had a girlfriend, and he was late to meet her, and even though it was almost dark and he knew he shouldn't be cutting through the park with all of the crap that was going on, he was doing it anyway.

But not because he wanted to see that girl.

Although he was running late, he could count on the fact that Heather would be at least twenty minutes later and that she would show up with a noisy entourage. She would be all out of breath and apologize fervently for being late, as though her lateness depended on such a rare and extenuating matrix of once-in-a-lifetime circumstances that it could never possibly happen again. And the next time she would be just as late.

He should just tell her it bugged him. He was basically a punctual person, and he didn't appreciate all the dramatic entrances. He didn't love the entourage, either.

But if he did tell her, she would probably listen and stop, at least for a while. And then where would he be? What could he complain about? What reason would he have for breaking up with her?

Ooh. That last bit just slipped out. He hadn't totally meant to have that thought.

Heather was gorgeous. Heather was smart. Heather was confident and funny. Heather, though only a senior in high school, was the envy of all his college friends. Heather was even capable, when she let go of her own mythology for a few minutes, of being a decent person.

But these were not good reasons for going out with a person, and he knew that in his heart. So why did he stay with her?

That was complicated. It hinged on a lot of stuff about his old life and his old self, and he didn't feel like thinking about it just now.

His thoughts wandered back to the girl. *The girl.* He'd certainly never thought so much about a person whose name he didn't know. His mind slipped back to her every time he gave it a moment's freedom. He kept picturing her eyes, infinite as the sky. His mind used to be so obedient, so precise. For the last twenty-four hours it had behaved more like a badly trained dog on a too long leash.

Did she live in the neighborhood? Where did she go to school? Would she come back to the chess tables in the park? If she did, would he try to talk to her? Would he ask her to play again?

His heart rate was rising at the very thought.

Okay, enough.

He was so distracted, he veered off the path and nearly crashed into a sign. He looked up at it.

Curb Your Dog, it said.

A Mistake

IF SHE SAW HIM, SHE WOULD just change course. Gaia's eyesight was good. She would spot him before he spotted her, before any interaction needed to take place.

Strictly speaking, walking through the park wasn't the smartest way to avoid him. But it was the fastest way to get home after she dropped Ed off at his house. And now that it was dark, it was by far her best chance for getting jumped or slashed by one of those neo-Nazi bastards.

She wasn't going to go out of her way for this guy.

Usually the park was still busy at this hour when the weather was good, but tonight it was nearly deserted. People were spooked by the reports of slashing. Lots of kids had been talking about it in school that day.

Gaia paused to take off her jacket and tie it around her waist. Slashing was such a random, mean-spirited brand of violence and the whole Nazi mythology so profoundly hateful, she was particularly eager to draw it out. She liked to think of herself as a trap. A walking trap.

As she dawdled in the wooded area near the dog run, she heard whispers. Oh, man. Could it be this easy? She strained her ears to hear and ambled a tiny bit closer. She couldn't really make out the conversation, but she did see the flash of a knife. Not a blade this time, a real knife. Four guys were huddled together, probably plotting their next attack.

Me! Me! Choose me! she thought. Jeez, what a wacko she'd become. She made as much noise as possible while still appearing naive and oblivious. She really hoped none of them would recognize her from a previous run-in.

She walked as slowly as she could without actually stopping and yet within moments found herself on the open, brightly lit sidewalk of Washington Square West untouched. So it wasn't her lucky night. Maybe tomorrow.

She felt sulky and suddenly quite alone. It was weird, this business of having a friend, she decided, thinking of her long, aimless walk with Ed. It made being alone less fun.

Gaia looked up and saw a figure crossing the street toward her. It was a girl, and she appeared to be heading straight into the park. Gaia's mind flashed to the knife she'd just seen, and she bent her steps toward the girl. She didn't realize until she was a few feet away exactly which girl it was.

"Is that Gaia?" a not-friendly voice demanded.

It was Heather. This really wasn't Gaia's lucky night. Gaia was immediately struck by the fact that Heather was alone. Where was the famed boyfriend? Where were the adoring, fashionably dressed friends?

"Listen, Heather," she began matter-of-factly, "you probably shouldn't—"

Heather bristled and walked on. "Leave me alone, bitch."

Gaia wasn't sure what to do. Follow her? "Heather, I really don't think—"

"Get away from me," Heather snapped. "I don't care what you think."

Gaia had intended to be helpful, but now she was angry. Let the stupid girl get slashed. It wasn't Gaia's responsibility. If anybody deserved it, Heather did.

Gaia's temper smoldered as she continued across the

street. She was just about to turn onto Waverly when she spotted more familiar faces. They were all three Heather acolytes. One was named Tina, she believed. The other was a girl whose name she didn't know, and the third was the good-looking guy from the cafe.

This time she was just going to keep walking, but one of them stopped her.

"You're Gaia, right?" the non-Tina girl asked.

"Yeah."

"Have you seen Heather, by any chance?"

Gaia looked from one to the next. This didn't seem like a trick or anything. "Yeah, I just saw her about a minute ago. She was cutting through the park." Gaia gestured in the general direction.

"Thanks," they all said. They weren't oozing warmth, but they seemed perfectly friendly.

"Hey, uh . . . Tina," Gaia called over her shoulder.

They all stopped and turned.

"You really shouldn't go through the park. There's a bunch of whacked-out guys in there, and at least one of them has a knife."

Tina and her friends looked surprised and alarmed in varying degrees. "Shit. Okay. Right."

"Thanks," the guy said again.

Gaia watched with satisfaction as they skirted the park, staying on the lighted sidewalk.

See? She'd done her good deed. She wasn't a bad person. She could go home in peace.

Sometimes I dream I'm skating. Not a ramp or half pipe like one of those Mountain Dew commercials. My feet are planted on a board, and I'm steaming along straight and steady. First it's maybe a sidewalk and then a street and then it becomes a highway of at least four lanes. Then the board transforms into an airplane, and I'm in the cockpit. It's a passenger plane, I guess, but I'm not aware of having responsibility for any passengers. I have this sense of excitement and anticipation as I accelerate, gaining intense, powerful speed. Fast, fast, faster. I feel sure I've passed that speed you need to leave the ground. But I'm still on the highway. I'm still zooming past houses and fields and forests.

The highway bends slowly into a curve. It curves again. I become conscious of road signs—Deer Crossing, Boulders Falling, you know those. And I begin to pay attention to them. I realize I've adjusted my speed from about a million miles an hour to just a few above the speed limit. I peer into the side mirror of my airplane to check for cops.

After a while it's a forgone conclusion that I won't be taking off. Just a plain fact, like any of the others we learn to live with. I'll be following signs on the highway in my jumbo jet, built to fly thirty-five-thousand feet above our blue Earth.

And she
followed
them through
the exit,
distinctly
aware of
the huge
cloud of
hate
behind
her.

no

peace

An Angry Place

BEFORE HE PASSED THROUGH THE school entrance the next morning, Ed knew there was something wrong. The halls were extra crowded, but not loud enough. Kids were gathered in little clots held together by hushed voices. A lot of eyes were darting around. The air had that heightened energy, that guilty pleasure of tragedy.

"What's going on?" he asked the first person he came to, a vaguely familiar girl with a magenta crew cut.

"God, it's so scary," she said. He could tell she was trying to rein herself in to project the right amount of sobriety. "Heather Gannis got shot in Washington Square last night. She's in the ICU at St. Vincent's."

"Jesus," Ed muttered. That sick zingy feeling, as if his blood were suddenly carbonated, started under his stomach and spread through his limbs. "Do they know who did it?"

The girl was already gone, so he wheeled up to the nearest group. "What happened? Who did it? Is she going to be okay?" he burst in loudly. He didn't feel like being measured and coy.

The five faces above him were practically caricatures of gravity. "The police claim they have suspects, but there hasn't been an arrest," a black-haired girl answered. "Nobody knows exactly what happened. They think it was some kind of gang activity—this white supremacist group—connected to the slashings."

"But it was a shooting," he argued.

"No, it wasn't. It was a stabbing," a guy said.

"A stabbing?" Ed asked.

At least two of them nodded.

"She's in ICU?" Ed continued, feeling impatient. He needed this information to slow his speeding heart. He actually cared about the facts and their implications, unlike most of the rumormongers.

"In a coma," another girl added.

He sighed in frustration. "We're talking about Heather?"

Black-Haired Girl's face closed in annoyance. "Obviously," she snapped.

Ed wheeled away, shaking his head. He had a feeling that if he talked to every one of the groups in the hallway, he would get a slightly different story from each.

This was surreal and terrifying. Heather wasn't the kind of girl who got shot or stabbed or stepped into a hospital for any reason but to visit her grandmother after elective surgery. He couldn't help but think of Heather's parents and sisters.

His experience on Mercer Street with Gaia came

back to him in full detail—the knife, the fear, the chaos. How had the world become so malignant? New York City was transforming from the eccentric but comfortable place where he'd grown up into the dangerous, angry place he'd always heard about.

"Attention, students." Principal Hickey's voice came blasting through the loudspeaker. "There will be an all-school assembly this morning directly after homeroom. Attendance is mandatory." Even the principal's solemnity sounded phony and exaggerated.

Ed wheeled slowly to homeroom, his mind ricocheting from big, appropriate thoughts about crime and death and police investigations to weird little inappropriate thoughts like whether Heather was wearing one of those hospital gowns that tied in the back, and, if so, who had undressed her. Then he felt guilty about having that second category of thoughts and tried not to have them, which took up a certain amount of mental energy in itself.

He was sitting in homeroom, trying not to have any thoughts at all, when he overheard Gaia's name mentioned. He didn't turn because he didn't want to disrupt the conversation.

"Gaia Moore saw what?" asked Becca Miller, a girl with long, supercurly hair who always sat behind him.

"She saw the guy with the knife in the park," responded Samantha something, a friend of Becca's, in a voice hushed but intoxicated with the thrill of conveying important information.

"What are you talking about?" Becca asked.

"Gaia was in the park just a few minutes before Heather got slashed, and she saw the guys who did it."

"Tell me you're kidding. How do you know this?" Becca demanded.

"Tina Lynch told Carrie she was with Brian and Melanie last night and they saw Gaia, right outside the park. Gaia told Tina she'd just seen Heather going into the park. But Gaia warned Tina and those other guys not to go into the park—that she'd just seen a guy with a knife."

Ed's mind was spinning with the number of names and personal pronouns, but also with the ramifications of what he was hearing. Gaia was involved. Of course she was. *If trouble was magnetic north, then Gaia's head was a huge chunk of iron.* In the short time Ed had known her, he'd almost gotten killed, watched three thugs get demolished, witnessed two catfights, seen one slashing victim's family crying on the news, and now learned his ex-girlfriend was in a coma.

Of course Gaia was there. How could it be otherwise?

But what had she done, exactly?

He couldn't trust these girls or really anybody but Gaia to tell him what had happened. And Gaia would give him the unvarnished truth. He and Gaia were alike in that way. They both took special satisfaction in telling you the one true thing you really, really didn't want to hear.

A Smelly Monster

GAIA HADN'T PAID MUCH ATTENTION to all the whispering at first. She had learned to be good at ignoring it. In her experience whispering either:

1. Didn't include her

or

2. Was about her

And in neither case could she take part.

So it wasn't until the assembly that she heard the news.

"As many of you know, a tragedy befell our school community last night," Principal Hickey intoned to the enormous, totally silent all-school assembly. Gaia should have known right then that something was seriously wrong by the simple fact that people were actually listening to the guy. "Heather Gannis was slashed in Washington Square Park last night. She lost a great deal of blood before she was discovered by friends and fellow students. She is in critical condition at St. Vincent's Hospital. I know you all join me in sending Heather and her family our . . ."

He kept talking, of course, but Gaia didn't hear. An ugly, evil creature with smelly fur and sharp fangs was gnawing on her intestines, and that was hard to ignore.

Her thoughts from the previous night returned to her word for word.

Let the stupid girl get slashed. If anybody deserved it, Heather did.

But I didn't mean that, a small, panicky voice inside Gaia claimed pitifully. I meant to warn her. I was going to, but—

Shut up! Gaia screamed at her own mind. If she'd had a tire iron, she would have clubbed herself with it. She'd heard too many excuses in her life. She couldn't stomach them, especially not from herself.

The principal was droning on about safety precautions now, and the attention he'd commanded was lost. Kids were talking, whispering.

Gaia realized when she looked up that hundreds of eyes were bouncing around and landing on her again and again. What could she expect? She had known exactly what Heather was walking into, and at least three other people in this very auditorium knew that she knew. She could have saved Heather, and she didn't. She let a petty, stupid conflict, probably based more on her own jealousy than anything else, destroy another person's life.

The fanged creature devoured several more feet of intestine and moved on to the lining of her stomach.

Everybody was standing up and milling around. Gaia guessed that the assembly was over. Numbly she got to her feet and let herself be moved along by the crowd. Just beyond the doors, in the lobby of the auditorium, the puffy, tear-stained face of Tina Whats-her-name bobbed into view.

Gaia stopped.

If only shame were part of fear. If only self-loathing were part of fear.

If Gaia were a better person, she would have offered some comforting words. She didn't. She remained the person she was.

"What *happened* last night?" Tina asked her in a voice tinged with hysteria. "What was Heather *thinking* going in there alone? Did you talk to her? Did you tell her what you'd seen in the park?"

Gaia realized Tina wasn't judging her. Not yet. She was inviting Gaia to commiserate, to take part in the why-oh-why-oh-why that churned her restless mind. She wanted to think the best of Gaia.

Other people had gathered. Some were comforting,

others being comforted. Several friends clutched Tina supportively.

"I—I didn't," Gaia said stiffly. "I didn't warn her."

Tina's face took a few moments to register this. "What do you mean?"

Gaia had to remind herself to breathe. "I mean I didn't tell Heather about the guy with the knife."

"Why not? Why didn't you?" Tina's shiny doe eyes turned into slitted bat eyes.

The crowd of people readied their looks of horror but held off, waiting for an explanation.

A part of Gaia wanted to describe to all these eager sets of ears how Heather told her off, called her names, but she knew it would sound just like the lame excuse it was. She deserved the blame for this. She would take it without flinching. "I just didn't."

Tina was crying now. "God, what's the matter with you? You warned us but not her? Do you hate Heather so much that you wanted her to get killed?"

Amid the loathing, judging faces, Gaia suddenly spied blue. Dark blue uniforms, dark blue hats. The fragments resolved into two policemen.

Could you actually get arrested for failing to warn someone? Gaia wondered irrationally. The faces parted to let the police come through. The hum of voices in the lobby grew to a roar.

"Are you Gaia Moore?" one of them, a tall black man, asked.

"Yes," she answered. Were they going to handcuff her right here, in front of the entire student body?

"Would you please come with us to the precinct? We have some questions to ask you."

The man asked it like a real question, not a rhetorical one. He waited for her answer; he didn't slap on any handcuffs.

"Yes," she said. "Of course." And she followed them through the exit, distinctly aware of the huge cloud of hate behind her.

That was one plus about profound self-loathing. Nobody could hate you worse than you hated yourself.

Differen but the Same

"AND AT APPROXIMATELY WHAT hour did you see Heather Gannis approaching the park from the west side?"

Gaia couldn't quite pull her eyes from that vague middle distance to focus them on the detective sitting across from her.

"About seven forty-five, I guess."

"You guess?"

"I wasn't wearing a watch at the time. I'd dropped off a friend at First Avenue and

Fourth Street at seven-thirty and then walked directly to the park on my way home. I figure it would take roughly fifteen minutes to walk from First and Fourth to Washington Square West," Gaia replied. She was on auto-answer. It felt to her that she'd already fielded at least a hundred thousand questions, and they hadn't even gotten to the meaty part.

"Fine. And what exactly happened when you saw Heather?" the detective asked. Detective Anderson was his name. He was in his forties probably, with thinning medium-brown hair, slightly pocked skin, and pale eyes. He looked just as tired and harassed as detectives always looked on those realistic cop shows.

Gaia let out her breath slowly. Did he really want the catty details? "I—um—sort of stopped her, and she—uh—" Gaia broke off and glanced at the detective. "See, Heather and I weren't exactly on friendly terms. A few days ago I spilled hot coffee on her, and since then—"

"Since then?" he prompted.

"We've had, uh, words, you could say," Gaia explained.

"I see." The detective nodded. "So you disliked Heather, did you?"

"I was told she is still alive."

"Excuse me. I'm sorry. Yes." Detective Anderson looked genuinely awkward. "You dislike Heather," he amended.

"That's a tough thing to say about a girl in a coma, sir," Gaia pointed out.

"Right. Yes. Okay." He sighed and shifted in his chair. "But as of yesterday evening, you and Heather were enemies?"

"Am I a suspect in this case?" Gaia asked, staring him dead in the eye.

He cleared his throat and shifted again. He moved his mouth a few times before any sounds came out. "Uh, no. You're not."

"Okay." She settled back in her chair. She knew she wasn't a suspect, because she knew they'd assembled a police lineup, because she'd overheard it being discussed when Detective Anderson was hunting around for cream for his coffee. She knew he was trying to pretend like she was so he could manipulate and intimidate her more easily.

"So, back to the story," she said, chilly but helpful. "Heather told me to leave her alone, and I did. Less than a minute after walking past her, I ran into her friends—Tina and two other people whose names I don't know. I think you know the story from there. After that I walked home. You have all that information already."

Detective Anderson looked even more harassed and tired. "Right. Now am I to understand that you did not warn Heather as to what you'd just seen moments before in the park?"

"No, sir."

"But you did warn the three people you saw subsequently?"

"Yes, sir."

He waited for an explanation that didn't come. After a while he stood up. "All right, Gaia, that's it for the moment. Would you come with me? I'd like you to look at a lineup."

She followed him through the precinct to the viewing room, listening to directions, warnings, assurances associated with a lineup. She felt floaty and distant as she took in the hodgepodge of beat-up office furniture, papers, files, boards, maps, clippings, notices, charts, the pathetic set of twigs on a windowsill that had probably been a live plant a decade or two ago.

It was so different in particulars, but so generally the same as the precinct where she'd spent the night as a twelve-year-old in San Rafael, California, after her mother was murdered, when they couldn't figure out anyplace else to put her.

"GAIA! GAIA! ARE YOU OKAY?"

Her Fault

It was Ed, waiting outside the police station for her, and she wasn't happy to see him. Who ever said misery loved company? Her misery did not love company. Her misery loved to be alone. Her misery threatened to bludgeon company.

"I'm fine." She hardly stopped. Another funny thing about having friends was that they expected things of you. They made you want to not be a terrible, awful, execrable person. They made you feel even worse when you were one. It was a lot easier not to have any friends.

"Gaia, wait. What's going on?" He rolled along after her.

She was tempted to find a quick set of stairs to ascend. Jesus, she really was an awful person.

"Haven't you heard from the angry hordes at school? I put Heather in the hospital. Didn't they tell you?"

"They—I—I mean—," Ed stammered.

"Come on, Ed. They did, didn't they?"

"But Gaia, you know it's not true," Ed argued, breathless from rushing to keep up with her. "You are not responsible for Heather. Even if you had warned her to stay away from the park, she would have cut through, anyway. She wouldn't have listened to you. There's nothing you could have done."

Gaia made a sharp turn onto West Fourth. Ed's tires practically left skid marks.

"Gaia, are you even listening?" Ed demanded.

She didn't bother to stop at the light on Seventh Avenue.

"Gaia! Come on!"

She practically sprinted all the way down Perry Street and pulled up short in front of George and Ella's house.

"Listen to me. What happened to Heather was scary and horrible, but it was not your fault."

Gaia walked up all fifteen steps of the front stoop before she turned around to look at him. "Ed Fargo. Thank you for trying beyond all possible reason to be my friend," she said quietly. "But it was my fault."

She turned her key in the door, went inside the house, and shut the door firmly behind her. She went up three flights of stairs with the grace of a robot. Once in her room she walked straight to the vintage turntable she'd recently hauled from the garbage and set up on the mantel. She reached behind the pile of records she kept in the nonfunctional fireplace to the LP in the very back.

She'd long ago memorized every centimeter of the faded, brittle record cover, memorized every word. She took out the record gingerly and set it on the player. She didn't need to study the grooves to know exactly where to set the needle.

The music filled the room, loud enough to destroy the speakers, to infuriate Ella, to explode her own head.

It was the second movement of the Sibelius violin concerto, the darkest, saddest piece of music on the planet. It was her mother's favorite—her weird, beautiful Eastern European mother with the embarrassing accent. Her mother knew all of Tchaikovsky, Rachmaninoff, Sibelius, and Prokofiev and nothing of Nirvana or any music Gaia held to be important at the time. She'd been so annoyed at her mother for that.

But now the soaring, wailing violin touched Gaia's cracked heart, and she did something she only allowed herself once or twice a year.

She lay down on the floor and cried.

He needed to pull himself out of this trance, to get a little distance.

the opposite of love

Not Thinking of an Elephant

SAM SAT IN THE WAITING ROOM OF the intensive care unit, rhythmically whacking his heel against the foot of the couch. It was just like hospital waiting rooms were supposed to be: genuine Naugahyde couch and chairs, plastic side tables displaying magazines you wouldn't have wanted to read in the late eighties when they came out. A mounted television showed some wretched soap opera that might as well have been filmed and closed-captioned in that very hospital.

He hadn't seen Heather since last night, and he felt nervous. Finding her in the park eighteen hours before, white as the moon in a dark puddle of blood, was such a potent jolt to his system, he was still breathing, moving, thinking too fast.

God, she'd looked so fragile and broken. He'd thought she was dead until he detected the faintest, slowest flutter of a pulse in her wrist. After that everything exploded into sound and motion. Screaming ambulance sirens, police sirens, people hurrying every which way.

He hadn't slept since, of course, so his senses were oddly distorted—colors were too bright, noises too shrill, smells too acrid. Time was disjointed. For example, hadn't it been at least two hours since Heather's parents had disappeared with a doctor into Heather's room, telling him they would be out in ten minutes?

What little peace he had would be shattered when Heather's sisters arrived from their colleges and Heather's friends stormed the place the moment school let out. A bunch of those friends had already camped out in the waiting room through their lunch period, spewing millions and trillions of words.

But Sam would suffer them. He would deprive himself of food and drink and sleep and continue to torture himself with this ridiculous soap opera as punishment, laughably slight though it was.

What was the punishment for? For contemplating a breakup with Heather not half an hour before she nearly bled to death. For sitting here, his skin intact as a newborn's, while Heather lay slashed in a coma. For thinking nonstop of *that girl.*

Mistake. Big mistake. Better not to think of thinking about her because then suddenly he was thinking of her. No. Stop. Heel. New thought.

New thought . . . He dragged his mind back to an absorbing topic, one he could worry and fiddle with obsessively, like a bloody hangnail. What was that girl's name? The one Tina and Co. had blathered on about for a solid hour? Maia. No. What was it? Gaia? Something like that. How he hated her. Loathed and despised her. What kind of person would let an innocent girl walk straight into a situation they knew was deadly? How petty and small and cowardly this girl Gaia must be.

Of course, the knife-wielding devil who attacked Heather deserved the real blame. But he was beyond hating. He was beyond imagining. Gaia, on the other hand, was a classmate. She was one of them.

Ah. This was good. Righteous indignation got him back on course every time. If he could just keep this focus, keep railing loyally against Gaia, he wouldn't have to think for minutes at a stretch of *that girl.*

The Boyfriend

GAIA DREADED THIS WORSE THAN she would dread a group hug with Ella and George or thirty-three simultaneous root canals or even trying out for the cheerleading squad. But she would make herself do it. She would drag herself right up to the eighth floor of this hospital, past the bevy of Heather's friends who detested her, the desperate parents who were too broken up to care about her, the steadfast, adoring boyfriend who'd maybe take a nanosecond from his grieving to curse her name. It was the right thing for Gaia to do. The fact that she dreaded it so much only made it seem more necessary.

Gaia emerged from the elevator and hesitated in front of the nurses' station.

"You're a friend of Heather Gannis?" the orange-haired nurse asked without even looking up from her computer.

"I—"

"Waiting room on your left," the nurse said, still not looking up.

Gaia loitered another moment, feeling wrong about going to the waiting room under false pretenses. But what was she going to do, pour out her heart to the overburdened nurse? Like she'd care that Gaia dumped coffee on Heather or that Heather bitched her out at a party?

"Okay," Gaia said, as meekly as she'd ever said anything. "Thanks."

Walk. Walk. Walk, she ordered herself.

Okay, there they were, spilling out into the hallway. The Friends. When they saw her, would they make a scene right there in the waiting room? Throw stones? Burn her at the stake?

The first murderous glance came from Tina herself. Many others followed as Gaia attempted to slip past the too full room. The murmur of hushed conversation stopped.

Tina gaped at her but was apparently so appalled, she couldn't speak. Instead the good-looking boy who'd been with Tina last night, the old suede-jacketed star of Gaia's cafe fantasy, stepped in.

"Why are you here?" he demanded.

Why was she here? That was a good question.

Because it was the last place on earth she wanted to be?

Because self-flagellation was the only thing that felt right?

Gaia's real answer made her sound like a kiss-ass, so she didn't want to say it out loud: She was here because she wanted and needed to apologize to Heather, even if Heather couldn't hear. Gaia didn't want to pander to the crowd, and she wasn't looking for social resurrection. She was perfectly happy being a pariah. That was as comfortable to her as a pair of old shoes.

So, as often happened, she said nothing. She continued on her way down the hall without a particular plan in mind.

The second room on the right, through a wide-open doorway, was Heather's. Gaia drew in a sharp breath and quickly averted her eyes. She hadn't meant to go right there exactly. She hadn't imagined how Heather would look, frail as a bird, hooked up by scores of tubes to machines that dripped and machines that bleeped, shorn of the self-consciously cool clothing and the beauty that made it so much easier for Gaia to ridicule her. Gaia suddenly felt like throwing up.

There was something much, much worse than your enemy receiving praise, fame, and riches and living happily ever after with an exceptionally handsome guy: your enemy getting slashed in the park after you hoped it would happen.

Her eyes swept into the room again. There, as expected, she saw the dark head of The Boyfriend, bowed over Heather's prone, still body. Maybe he was crying.

Oh, shit. Shit. Shit. Gaia had no right to be there. What had she been thinking?

It was some selfish hope for exoneration that brought her, nothing nobler than that. Now what? She'd walk herself to the end of the hall. She'd wait a minute or two. She'd walk herself back out to the reception area, maybe find a waiting room on another floor, keep her own private vigil for a few hours—or days, if necessary—until things settled down. And then, as politely as possible, she'd apologize to Heather's parents and ask if she might have permission to apologize to Heather. They'd think she was a complete freak, but that hardly mattered, did it?

Gaia trudged to the end of the hall. On her way back she cast one last look in Heather's room. Quiet though she was, The Boyfriend chose that very moment to look up.

Gaia's eyes stuck to his, and she couldn't move them.

Her body reacted before her mind. Her head swam. The Coke she'd had for lunch climbed up her esophagus. All oxygen departed her lungs.

It was him. He was it.

It, him, he was Heather's boyfriend.

The evil, ugly monster with the matted, stinking hair and the razor-blade fangs moved up from her stomach and took a chomp at her heart.

Gaia staggered toward the elevator so he wouldn't see her when her knees gave out.

A Salted Slug

IN RETROSPECT, IT WOULD HAVE BEEN so much better if Sam had stayed where he was.

Instead, for no good reason, he allowed his unfaithful legs to carry him from Heather's side, where he belonged, down the hall and after *the girl*.

It was impossible for him to explain why. He didn't decide to do it. His body was just suddenly up and moving. It was like when the doctor thwacked your knee. You didn't *decide* to kick your foot.

"Wait," he said as she fled from him just as she had a few days before.

Heather's sisters and a crowd of friends blocked the hallway, impeding the girl's progress. She dodged and wove like a running back facing a defensive line.

"Leaving already, Gaia?" he overheard Carrie Longman say in an unmistakably hostile voice.

The girl broke through the line and made for the elevator bank. Sam followed her there along with a lot of whispers and nasty looks. It honestly did not occur to him that *the girl* was the girl Carrie had been addressing until he was facing her, just two feet away from her, in front of the elevators.

His thoughts were covered in molasses. They moved achingly slowly with big gaps between them.

The girl Carrie had been addressing was called Gaia. . . .

This girl he was now gaping at was called Gaia. . . .

This girl was *the girl*. . . .

The girl was Gaia. . . .

Gaia was the one who had . . .

"Y-You're Gaia," he said to her.

She was silent for a long time, just staring. Her eyes were too much for him.

"You're The Boyfriend," she said slowly.

It sounded like a felony, like an atrocity, the way she said it.

"Sam. My name is Sam."

"Oh." Her face was strangely open, her eyes a whirlpool.

He was scared to let himself read them this time. He was scared of getting sucked in.

"I—you—w-w-we—," he stammered. What exactly did he want to say?

He could see from the panel above the nearest elevator that it was climbing toward them. 3 . . . 4 . . . 5 . . .

"You're the Gaia who saw the guy with the knife in the park last night," he blurted out in a disorganized rush. "You're the one who didn't warn her."

The girl's face was a little too white for a person with a beating heart. Her hands trembled at her sides. She nodded.

"W-Why? I don't understand. Do you dislike her that much?"

"I—I guess I do."

Silence. 6 . . . 7 . . .

He needed to pull himself out of this trance, to get a little distance. He needed to remember who needed defending here. He looked away from her, summoning his shield of righteous indignation. "What is wrong with you? Are you some kind of monster?" He hated the way his voice sounded.

She took so long to respond, it was punishing. Those wide, boundless eyes pinned him to his spot with a look that made him feel horrible, like a salted slug.

"You're not what I thought," she said finally.

Why should *he* feel horrible? *He* hadn't done anything wrong.

The elevator arrived on eight. The doors opened with glacial slowness.

Suddenly he hated her. It was only partly rational, partly fair. She was the source of all the problems, of Heather's condition, of the shameful, disloyal thoughts that had invaded his brain. Now in her face, in her eyes, he saw none of the tenderness or the possibilities he saw before.

"I hate you," he said, amazed as the babyish words emerged from his own mouth.

She stepped into the elevator. "I hate you, too."

He watched her face until the doors closed.

Unbidden, that stupid saying entered his mind: that one about hate not being the opposite of love.

Cold Coffee

"WHO PICKED CJ OUT OF THE lineup?" the older woman asked, leaning over the table that divided them, resting her chin in her palm.

Marco could see down her lavender blouse to the tops of her breasts spilling out of a white bra with lace edges. He wanted to kiss her and touch her so bad. She always wanted to talk first. That was the way most girls were, in his experience. So his mouth went one way and his mind another.

"Nobody knows for sure. Some guys think it was that blond girl—that, uh, friend of yours. A couple of them saw her in the park last night before that other girl . . . you know." He didn't feel like going any deeper into this particular subject. He wanted to talk about how good her shiny red hair looked all loose like that and the dream of his she'd starred in last night.

She crossed her legs under the table, and her knee brushed his. "I heard on the news that the girl who was slashed—they didn't release her name—is out of a coma and expected to make a full recovery," she said.

"Yeah? That's good news for CJ. They'll stick him with assault instead of murder. He never meant to hurt her so bad."

"CJ's in custody? Nobody came up with bail?" she asked.

He pressed his shin against hers. "Nah. It was like a hundred grand or something. His mother lives in Miami. She doesn't even know about it."

"So maybe you'll need to take over in his absence?"

Marco lifted his shoulders so they looked extra big. "Yeah, that's the plan. Tarick, you know, Marty's older brother, wants me to, uh, take care of this old Jew foreigner in the park, this crazy guy who sits over by the chess tables."

She nodded and sipped her coffee.

Marco looked down at his own coffee. He'd hardly touched it. He'd only ordered it because it seemed more mature than a Coke. The coffee was cold now, and an iridescent grease slick quivered on the top. Everything in this diner was greasy, but the tables in back were private.

Why was she so fascinated by this stuff? Nothing seemed to shock her or upset her. Was she a writer for a magazine or something? Even though she was older, she was so freakin' sexy, he didn't care much as long as she changed the names and all that.

"Why the old guy?" she asked.

Marco shrugged. "'Cause he's there. He's kind of a joke in the park. This loser kid who wants to be part of things—Renny is his name—he loves this old guy. Marty and them think it would be funny."

"Are you going to do it?"

Marco smiled in a way he thought was both tough and mysterious. "I'll see."

She didn't smile back. "Do you want something else?" she asked. "A Coke?"

He couldn't wait anymore. He stood and grabbed her hand. "I want to get out of here."

She remained seated. "I want to finish my coffee."

1 poppy-seed bagel with cream cheese

1 large coffee with milk and 2 sugars

3 Wint-O-Green Life Savers

When I was twelve, my mind's eye would sometimes flash on excruciating images from the night I lost my mother. They destroyed me, but I couldn't stop. The worst thing you can do in that situation is order your mind *not* to think of something. You know, the old "don't think of an elephant" problem. So I invented these tactics for distraction.

The first line of defense was to think about kids at school. Not my friends, exactly, because I didn't have many of those, but the people I fantasized about being friends with. I'd weave these scenes filled with cute dialogue about the fun we'd all have palling around together.

The second line of defense was imagining a boy to fall in love with. What would he look like? What kinds of things would he say to me? Would it be love at first sight, or would it take me a few minutes to overwhelm him with my charm?

If those two didn't work, I exiled my mind to listing European capitals, which my dad made me memorize when I was three.

And finally, if my mind offered absolutely no place to hide, if thinking at all was sheer torment, I would distract it by cataloging what I'd eaten the day before.

Tonight, lying on the floor of my room, the first three attempts led to:

1. Heather
2. Sam
3. Belgrade

I skipped directly to yesterday's breakfast.

Sam was watching
the place across
the park where
Gaia's back had
been minutes
before.

"I don't know,"
he said
absently. "I
got distracted,
I guess."

the pretty one

HEATHER WAS GOING TO BE OKAY.

Heather was expected to make a full recovery.

Nuts

Gaia was so happy, she felt like telling the man behind the sandwich counter at Balducci's.

"Roast beef?" he asked her.

"Yes," she said. "On that." She pointed to an extravagant-looking roll.

It was all over school today, all anybody was talking about. That and the part Gaia played in the catastrophe. The way the rumor mill was spinning, Gaia expected she would be charged with the slashing herself before the end of the day.

And that was, admittedly, part of the reason why it was 11:45 A.M. and Gaia was buying a sandwich rather than listening to her imbecilic math so-called teacher botch an elementary explanation of sine and cosine.

She paid for the nine-dollar sandwich and headed down Sixth Avenue, swinging the green-and-white bag. Zolov would eat like a king today. She imagined his face when she surprised him at the unusual hour.

Cutting was a serious offense, as she'd been told a few thousand times. Ooooh. She pictured the vice principal calling George at work. Or, God forbid, Ella.

She almost skidded to a stop at a pay phone at the corner of West Eighth. She plunked in her quarter and dialed George's work number. "George Niven, please."

George's voice came on a few seconds later. "This is George Niven."

"Hi, George, it's Gaia. How's it going?"

"Just fine, Gaia. Just fine." He sounded surprised and pleased. "You sound like you're . . . uh . . ."

"I'm actually calling from a pay phone, because I left school early, because I wasn't feeling well."

"I'm sorry to hear that." His voice was filled with such genuine concern, she felt a little bad. "Did you speak to—"

"It's nothing serious. It's . . . well, you know, it's *that* time of the month, and I get these really bad cramps sometimes." Gaia knew there was no faster way to get a man off the phone than to bring up her period.

"Right, right. Of course. Understood." She'd never heard him talk so fast.

Poor George. It was hard enough having a girl in your house, let alone one who arrived fully formed at the age of seventeen.

"So, would you just give them a call and let them know what's up?" she asked.

George was clearly so traumatized, he didn't argue. "Yes. I'll give them a call at the . . . uh, office there. You, uh, just let Ella know. She'll take care of you. There's, uh, there's no better sick nurse than Ella."

Gaia almost laughed at that one. Ella's skirts were too tight to sit at a bedside, and she probably couldn't distinguish aspirin from arsenic. God help George. Love was more than blind. It was deaf and dumb, too. It was catatonic. It was vegetative.

Sixth Avenue passed her by in a stimulating buzz. The buses, the baby strollers, the three-man Peruvian band that played on the corner, the delis overflowing with fruit and flowers, the guy selling dirt-cheap tube socks, underpants, and secondhand books from a card table set up by the curb.

The world was fresher and a lot more spacious when you were supposed to be in school. Kind of like a public pool during adult swim.

She rounded the corner of West Fourth in eager anticipation. Maybe today she would buy a bag of those sugary roasted nuts. The exquisite smell was already reaching her nostrils. Yes, today would be the day.

She breezed into the park, actually appreciating the sunshine for once. It made the place seem so different from the malicious gang nest where Heather had been slashed. She saw Zolov's hunched, familiar back and almost ran for him.

Then she stopped short. She dropped the bag and watched the silver-foil-covered sandwich roll over hexagonal gray stones. She put her hand to her heart.

He was there. The Boyfriend. Sam. Whatever.

He was sitting directly across from *her* friend, concentrating on the chessboard. How dare he? Was he trying to hustle poor old Zolov? Couldn't he see the old man had nothing to lose besides his terrible coat and his Power Ranger? Shouldn't he be in school or something?

She hoped the old man would summon up all his skill and beat the crap out of him.

The Boyfriend, Sam, whatever, looked scruffier today. The cuffs of his flannel shirt weren't buttoned, nor were they rolled up. His hair was sticking up a little in back, and his eyes looked tired. Probably from staying up all those hours worrying about Heather.

Blah. *Blah.* The thought made her sick.

Gaia grabbed the sandwich and stuffed it back in the bag. Now what? She didn't want to see him or talk to him, but she didn't want to flee like a little mouse, either.

Of course he had to look up right then. Right then, as she clutched her pathetic green-and-white bag, paralyzed with uncertainty, eyes round and startled.

Why did he have this effect on her? Why? Had she some intuitive knowledge, the day they played chess, that he was Heather's boyfriend? Did she recognize he represented the best possible way to torment herself?

She couldn't be having these alien feelings about Heather's boyfriend. It was too cruel a coincidence. Was somebody up there having a belly laugh at her expense?

Her mind flashed back to their last encounter in the hospital, and she wanted to groan out loud. She felt her cheeks turning warm.

No doubt about it. She was a femme fatale. A romantic heroine for the ages. A heartbreaker. A female

James Bond. A role model for girls everywhere.

Of the two boys Gaia had ever met in her *entire life* who could have possibly ever maybe meant something important to her (and coincidentally, the only two who had ever beaten her in chess—Stephen from around the corner being the first), she'd told them both she hated them. She was two for two.

No wonder she'd never kissed anybody. "I hate you" wasn't exactly come-hither. It wasn't a big turn-on to most guys. Not ones who belonged on this side of prison, anyway.

Maybe she could sell a book touting her romantic advice. *Gaia's Rules.* Not only should you not call the sucker back; go ahead and tell him you hate him.

And as a follow-up she could publish her popularity secrets. Okay, it was time to go somewhere else. Time to let up on the mean-yet-indifferent laser beams she was directing from her eyes.

She wheeled around, sandwich bag in hand, and walked toward the fountain. It was a beautiful, warm day. Why didn't she just go to the fountain? That was a normal thing to do.

The benches were filled with mothers of babies, nannies, college students, people who didn't have jobs. There, directly in front of her, bathed in the buttery shade of a yellow umbrella, stood the pushcart filled with nuts so sugary and delicious, the smell alone could make you hallucinate.

And she was going to buy a bag. So what if her stomach felt like it had been stapled shut?

"One bag, please," she said to the cart's proprietor as he stirred the caramelized mass. She thrust two dollars in his hand, and he gave her the warm, paper pouch filled with sticky nuts. The smell was a living thing. She put one in her mouth. She chewed. She tried another.

She kept chewing as she walked herself from the fountain to the dog run near the perimeter of the park, feeling her hopes deflate as the grease from the nuts soaked through the paper to her fingers.

Sugar-roasted nuts, as it turned out, could be added to the list that included vanilla extract and bread and meeting a guy you could fall in love with—things that smelled a lot better than they tasted.

"CHECKMATE."

Six Minutes and a Pawn

Sam glanced up in surprise. Zolov wasn't looking at him with his usual winking smile of triumph. He was looking at him with pity.

He had lost? Already? How could that be?

Of course, he always lost to Zolov. In spite of his

insanity, Zolov was a truly great player. In his day the old guy had beaten or drawn many of the greatest chess players in the world. But usually Sam and Zolov fought their way through long, dramatic battles, masterful exchanges of material. Today it was six minutes and a pawn.

"Vhat happened to you?" Zolov asked.

Sam was watching the place across the park where Gaia's back had been minutes before. "I don't know," he said absently. "I got distracted, I guess."

"By zat geerl?"

Sam couldn't breathe. He was choking. Was it possible to choke to death on your own saliva? "W-Who?"

"Za preetty vun. She's smart, too, you know."

"I—uh—I don't know who you mean."

Zolov was now smiling. "I teenk you do."

Sam almost bit his tongue in annoyance. After two years of listening to Zolov theorize about the young man who sold sodas by the fountain (World War I Polish spy called Tuber), the social worker from the homeless coalition (malevolent alien from a whole other solar system), the old man picked quite a moment to be perceptive.

"I gotta go," Sam said, standing. "Good game," he lied, handing Zolov a five. "I'll see you Thursday."

"Sam?"

Sam turned around in amazement. Zolov called

him "boy" and "keed" and "you," but he never called him "Sam."

"Yeah?"

"You go get zat geerl and tell heer I vant my sand-veech."

"No way," Sam muttered to himself. No way was he ever going anyplace near that kind of trouble again.

As a child, I was a disaster. I had a terrible stammer, which made me shy and pitifully awkward. My teeth pointed in every direction, and my hair was so thick, it lay in a stack on my head.

It started early. I was a maladjusted baby. You may think all babies are at least a little bit cute, but I wasn't. I didn't walk till after I was two. I don't think I learned to talk at all until I was four years old.

My stammer was triggered by everything but by nervousness most of all, and I was always nervous. It was your classic catch-22: My nervousness made me stammer, and the more I stammered, the more nervous I got. I even stammered in my thoughts.

I was badly isolated. I spent all my time either on the computer or playing chess. Or playing chess on the computer. I started playing in chess tournaments when I was about six. Even

among chess geeks I was considered untouchable. Stop by a chess tournament sometime, and you will see how truly scary that is.

I have an older brother to remind me of all this, in case I ever forget.

When I was twelve, my parents started to worry about me in earnest. I suspect they were embarrassed to take me anyplace. I had a crash course in speech therapy. Several, to be honest. A vengeful orthodontist installed an aircraft carrier worth of metal in my mouth. My mom dragged me to a haircutter who cost about a thousand dollars. She outfitted me at the Gap.

By the time I returned to school for seventh grade, I was unrecognizable. I actually considered changing my name and just starting from scratch.

So I guess you could say life as I know it began when I was twelve. I was born that first day of junior high.

I'm fine now. Even good, according to a lot of people. I know how to dress. I know how to speak. And even so, I'm still good at chess.

I masquerade as one of the blessed. One of the normal, effortless joiners who believe, without thinking about it too deeply, that the world exists for people like us. It's a lie, of course. I come from the other side. I know what it's like over there.

There are still vestiges of dorkdom in me. (See my use of the word *vestiges*, for example.) They pop up all the time. They remind me that if I were born in another age, say, prehistory—before braces and speech therapy—I would be the dorkiest caveman who ever lived. And the person I was probably meant to be.

Her gaze swept over Sam's still body, and she had an almost overwhelming need to go to him, to kneel over him and make sure he was breathing.

melting away

First and Second Punches

SHE WASN'T *THAT* PRETTY. OKAY, she was that pretty. But not pretty like Heather—the kind of pretty that everybody noticed right away. Gaia's face, devoid of makeup or any expression meant to please, was unfortunately more mesmerizing to Sam every time he saw it. God, and those eyes. They haunted him. He couldn't get a fix on them—one time they were the endless azure of a summer sky, another time the blue-violet of early evening, and still another the indescribable color of a typhoon.

He turned up LaGuardia. It was almost eight-thirty in the evening, and he wanted to get to the hospital to see Heather before visiting hours were up. He'd cut through the park. Just a corner of it.

But it wasn't just the way Gaia looked. Was it because she was so unbelievably good at chess? Granted, that had really thrown him. But that couldn't explain it fully, either.

He had every reason to dislike her. He *did* dislike her. No decent person would have treated Heather the way Gaia had. For a while he'd tried convincing himself that he was thinking about her so much because he disliked her, but it wasn't working anymore.

Sam was a rational person. Overly rational,

if you listened to Heather, or his mother, or most of his friends. He wasn't romantic. He wasn't poetic. He wasn't nostalgic. He wasn't obsessive—until this week, anyway. What was wrong with him? What were the chances that she, Gaia, had thought about him even a minute for each hour he'd thought of her?

He was a rational person. He would figure this out, and maybe then he could make it go away, he assured himself as he glanced toward the chess tables, squinting through the darkness to see that none of the few shadowy figures was hers.

He didn't see her, but he did see something strange. He moved closer.

He first recognized the hunched shape of Zolov swaying to get to his feet. Another figure was hovering, bearing down on the old man. He heard a groan, first quiet, then it grew loud and terrifying. Sam was running before he was able to process what was happening.

"Zolov!" he shouted.

The old man was waving his arms, trying to defend himself from the attack. He shouted hoarsely in a language Sam didn't understand.

It was a young man, Sam realized as he raced toward them, and he had a razor blade.

"Get away from him!" Sam shouted.

The young man turned his head and locked eyes with Sam for a millionth of a second. He was young, dark haired, intense, pumped up on adrenaline or something else. Sam hated him. What kind of monster would attack a fragile, crazy old man? Sam watched in horror as he threw Zolov to the ground.

Zolov cried out. Sam saw blood on the old man's face, flooding the crags and wrinkles. His heart was seized with panic. He threw himself at the attacker and shoved him as hard as he could. Thoughts were only fragments moving through his mind at uneven speeds. The attacker lost his balance, but only for a moment. He steadied himself and came at Sam.

There was a fist, really big. Sam heard an awful-sounding crack, then saw the orange insides of his eyelids. He blinked his eyes open. He was still on his feet. His cheekbone was blazing with pain. One eye was pounding, already swelling with blood.

The fist was coming again, but time was 0slow now. Slow enough for Sam to dodge the fist and to remember that he had never been in a fight before, that he was out of his league. He willed his hand to clench. He trained his good eye on the guy's mouth. He swung as hard as he could.

His knuckles connected to soft flesh. The guy grunted. Sam felt a surge of energy so strong, it seemed to erase his memory, to blow out his consciousness. He swung again without thinking. He caught an ear this time, hard. The guy staggered to one side, caught his balance. He didn't come back at Sam, as Sam was expecting. Instead he stepped backward, putting several more feet between them.

"You're dead," he hissed at Sam through blubbery, swollen lips. "I'm going to kill you." And then he ran off.

Sam was almost instantly kneeling at Zolov's side. The old man was groaning softly. Sam took his shirt and gently wiped away blood so he could determine the seriousness of the wound. It appeared to be shallow and less than two inches in length but bleeding heavily. Zolov's eyes fluttered open, then shut again. His breath was short and raspy. Sam was suddenly terrified the old man's heart was going to stop. He hated to leave him, but he needed to get help.

"Zolov," he whispered, cradling his head. "You're gonna be okay, but I need to call an ambulance. I'll be back as fast as I can." He laid the gray, frizzled head on the soft ground. He stood looking at him for another moment before he took off at a sprint for the public pay phone.

Another Mistake

AS SOON AS GAIA HEARD THE NOISE the fine, light hair on her arms prickled and her skin was covered with bumps. She had the feeling sometimes that when she sensed danger, her vision and her hearing became almost supernaturally acute. She could almost feel her muscles feasting on oxygen, preparing for action. She knew the muffled cries and moans were Zolov's well before she actually saw him.

Zolov's attacker broke away as Gaia flew to the old man's side. She put her arms around the frail shoulders, examining the wound on his face. There was a certain amount of blood, but it was already thickening around the slash. That was a good sign. She clutched him gently. "You're going to be fine," she promised him, not wanting to leave him in his disoriented state.

But she had to because, amazingly, the demon who had attacked the old man was still within sight. Gaia ran like hell. In the darkness she saw nothing more than his silhouette.

The attacker sprinted toward the south edge of the park. Gaia flew after him, her rage undergoing nuclear fission as her feet pounded the pavement. What kind of monster would attack a helpless old man?

He was fast, but she was faster. She literally launched herself from the ground and tackled him from behind. He shouted in surprise. They rolled together across a grassy patch, limbs tangling. Strong arms circled her hips, pulling her down. They tumbled again before she managed to pin him under her. She secured his torso between her knees and shoved his head to the ground. Her hands were tightening around his neck before she looked him in the face.

She closed her eyes in disbelief. When she opened them again, her heart changed places with her stomach.

It was Sam.

She was so astounded, she let go of him, and in an instant he'd flipped her over. Now he was kneeling over her, pressing her shoulders into the ground with his hands.

"*Gaia*, what do you think you're *doing?*" he bellowed at her.

She saw clearly now that one of his eyes was purple and almost swollen shut. Her mind was whizzing, trying to make sense of it.

"Zolov is hurt," Sam yelled only inches from her ear. "He was slashed. I need to call for help!"

Her ears rang painfully. "Y-You," she choked out. "I thought you—"

"You thought I what? I slashed him? Are you insane?" Sam's eyes—or the one that was still open, anyway—were wild with adrenaline. Her waist was gripped too tightly between his knees. He was digging the heels of his hands into her chest.

In a lightning-quick move she managed to get one hand around each of his arms and pulled them out from under him. His weight collapsed on top of her, and she quickly flipped him over again. She drove her knee into his abdomen and held him steady with her forearms. "Then who did it?" she demanded.

He stared at her with a mixture of anger and disbelief. "Some asshole who's going to get away if you don't *get the hell off me!*" He wrapped his arms around her back in a bear hug and tried to roll her again, but this time she wasn't budging.

He was holding her so tight, her face was buried in his neck. "Fine," she said as well as she could, considering her lips were pressed against his skin. "Let me go, and I'll let you go." But neither of them moved.

"Fine. You let go first," he demanded in her hair. His voice was strained by the presence of her knee in his stomach.

Gingerly, slowly, she let up the pressure from her knee.

"Whoa!" she called out as he threw her off him, fast and surprisingly hard. Her butt landed on the pavement. "Ouch," she complained.

She was mad. She couldn't help herself. As soon as he was on his feet she sprang to hers and shoved him. He reeled backward a couple of steps, then leaped at her and shoved her right back.

Her eyes widened in disbelief. As soon as she caught her balance, she stormed at him. He was a lot taller than she, so she had to jump to jab her shoulder into his solar plexus.

"Uff!" he grunted. She was satisfied to see she'd

nearly knocked the wind out of him. She put two hands on his stomach and pushed him to the ground.

With admirable speed he rolled toward her and hugged her ankles. "Oh!" she shouted in surprise as he pulled her legs out from under her. She fell directly on top of him.

In anger and confusion she grabbed the first thing she could—his hair, as it turned out. He grabbed hers right back. She was lying on top of him, one arm around his neck. His legs were clasped around hers, his arm circling her waist.

Where had her great fighting prowess gone? She'd been baffled, confused, angered by this guy who wasn't extraordinarily skilled or trained. And now she'd been reduced to pulling hair?

"There he is!" a voice shouted.

From their tangle on the grass they both looked up, mute.

"OH, SHIT," SAM MUMBLED, STILL clutching Gaia as the guy who had attacked Zolov came near, flanked by two guys on each side. The guy's lips were grossly misshapen, and he looked mad enough to dismember, if not kill.

Suddenly Sam found himself holding Gaia even tighter, but strangely, his motive had transformed. He no longer wanted to pull her limb from limb; now he felt an urgent need to protect her.

There were five of them. Count them, five. Three of them were big. Two of them looked young—in their middle teens, maybe, and not totally filled out. For a moment he buried his eyes in Gaia's soft, pale hair.

If it weren't so surreal and horrendous, he would have laughed. In the last five minutes he'd thrown the first and second punches of his life, found himself wrestling on the ground with the object of his infatuation—not only brilliant at chess but a match for Hulk Hogan. Now he was holding her in his arms and smelling her hair as he faced imminent death at the hands of five angry gang members while his ancient friend and mentor was possibly bleeding to death.

"Get off your girlfriend and stand up," the slasher demanded roughly.

Somehow it didn't seem necessary to point out that Gaia was not his girlfriend. They sorted out their limbs and both stood up. They exchanged a look, filled with things he couldn't decipher. Amazing how quickly your enemy seemed like your friend when faced with a worse enemy.

"Jesus, it's *her,*" one of the guys said.

Sam looked at Gaia again. He couldn't guess what that meant. "Leave her alone," he barked at them, stepping forward. He suddenly felt like he was playing a role in a movie, portraying a character who said and did things he never would. Best to keep pretending because reality—namely five guys (and possibly one girl) who wanted to kill him—was hard to take.

"Gaia, go," he said in a low voice. "I'll be okay." Ha! Had his character really just said that? She was standing so close, he could still feel the warmth of her body. It was intoxicating—really not what he needed at the moment.

The guy, the swollen-lipped slasher, was only a few feet away now, bouncing a little on the balls of his feet. His friends had circled Sam and Gaia. Two of them wore floppy hoods, covering their shaved heads and keeping their faces in shadow. Another had a Doo-Rag pulled low over his forehead. As he looked at them Sam was weirdly calm and disconnected. He was resigned to getting beat up. He felt more scared about what they might do to Gaia.

"Let her go," Sam said.

The guy's smile was grotesque with the swollen lip pulling in odd directions. "My bud CJ thinks she did him wrong."

One of the hooded guys came forward and grabbed Gaia by the shoulders. He dragged her several yards from Sam, pinning her arms to her sides in a bear hug.

The horror was now dawning on Sam. He felt bile rising in his throat. Anger mixed with fear to make desperation. Gaia's eyes were huge and luminous.

He went after the guy who held her. Fast, without letting himself think too much, he hauled off and punched the guy, catching his jawbone so hard, his knuckles blazed. Gaia slipped quickly out of the guy's grip.

Get away, he urged her silently. Run away and get—

He'd grabbed her waist and was about to physically shove her when a slamming blow to the back of his head shattered his mind. He spun around and got a sharp kick in the stomach. He was lying on the ground now, disoriented by the number of arms and feet and faces spinning against a sapphire sky. A kick landed on his chest and took his breath away.

He saw Gaia's face over him, glowing white like an angel's. Broken thoughts and feelings lay in pieces, with edges sharp enough to cut. He reached for her. He wanted to tell her something, but he couldn't fit the aching, full-hearted feelings into words. The last thing he saw from the corner of his eye was a Timberland coming at the side of his head. After that, thankfully, he saw and felt nothing.

Sleeping Beauty

GAIA WASN'T AFRAID. SHE WAS never afraid. But she felt the abstract terror of a world without Sam, without the idea or the possibility of Sam, and she didn't want to live there. It felt so dark and arid that it would surely dry up all of her senses and parch her last blossom of hope.

Her rage exploded, less controlled, more intense than ever before. The five of them became an indistinguishable mass to her, without human features. She took them on as one multilimbed creature. Her adrenaline carried her, so she didn't have to think or count or predict.

She took one of them out with her fist. Clean, just like that. Another one required a combination of kicks to finish him off. In the process she took a sharp jab in the ribs and another guy's fist caught her in the forehead as she tried to duck. She could feel the blood gathering at the wound. The red drips were a nuisance in her eyes, but she was too far gone to feel pain.

Two of the guys bobbed in her peripheral vision. The third she had head-on in her sights. She planted a kick in that vulnerable place in his neck just as another one slammed her from the side. Another down, she registered as she tried to find her balance. Then came another slam from the side. The blood stung her eyes and tinctured her mouth with its coppery flavor. Head wounds bled too much. It was a shame. She might not have enough time.

Two weaving heads, eight thrashing limbs. It was an ugly but simpler creature that remained.

Her gaze swept over Sam's still body, and she had an almost overwhelming need to go to him, to kneel over him and make sure he was breathing.

Bam! A blow to her stomach sent her sprawling on the ground. *Focus, Gaia,* she urged herself. She had to focus as hard as she possibly could to get them through this. Loss of blood made her hazy and faint.

Another guy came rushing toward her at an angle she could use. She caught his momentum and threw him over her head. He rolled twice. It gave her enough time to get back to her feet. But just as she did the other one smashed her from behind and sent her back to the pavement. As she raised her head, she saw a pale, scared face peering from a stand of trees. She knew the face. He took a few steps forward.

"Renny, you little shit, get over here!" the bigger of the guys bellowed.

Renny was frozen, except for his face, which quivered like a squirrel's.

Suddenly Gaia felt her arms wrenched roughly behind her back. The two of them were holding her. She tried to jab her way free with her elbow, but she couldn't move it.

"Come on, little boy, here's your big chance!" the other guy called.

Gaia didn't feel like writhing to get out of their grip. It was a waste of time. The blood was leaving her head and making her feel tired. She wished she could just pass out and be done with it.

"Renny! Step up, man. You in or out?"

Renny took another step forward. He looked terrified at the sight of Gaia, no doubt something right out of a horror movie with all that blood on her face and shirt.

Suddenly Gaia saw the dull glint of steel. She thought she was imagining it at first. But even the idea was enough to clear her foggy head.

Yes, it was real. She could see it clearly now. The fat-lipped guy was pushing a gun, a .38-caliber pistol, into Renny's hand. Where had it come from? Why hadn't she been paying better attention? "Finish her off, Renny. Do it now!"

Gaia's adrenaline level notched up. Her body was on full alert, but her mind had entered that dreamlike state, wondering numbly, philosophically, whether this was the end of her life. There were few physical brawls she couldn't find her way out of, but a gun changed everything. It empowered the cowardly and rendered skill, bravery, and character useless.

That was why Gaia, though she was trained to be an exceptional markswoman, never used one. She'd rather lose on her terms than win on those. Now the gun was in Renny's hand. Shaky, but pointing directly at her. He wasn't looking anywhere near her eyes.

Oh, this was hard to take. Was little Renny, her favorite chess whiz, really going to sink a bullet into her? It seemed like a very bad life where that would happen. If he was going to, she hoped he would get on with it because she didn't feel like sticking around much longer to watch.

Renny looked like he was going to puke. His eyes were glazing over, and his skin was the color of iceberg lettuce. He came up so close, she could hear his breath. She was staring down the barrel of the gun. She pulled her eyes back to Renny's.

Look at me, she demanded of him silently. Look at me! *Look at me!* If he was going to do this, let him do it for real. Let him know the full meaning of popping that trigger.

Don't be a coward, Renny. Look at me!

At last he did. His eyes lighted on hers. He hesitated only a moment. Then he turned and ran like hell. Gaia heard the gun clattering on the pavement.

Good boy, Renny, she told him silently as he sprinted for the streetlights.

"Freakin' coward," one of the guys muttered.

It gave Gaia the burst she needed. She slammed her heel as hard as she could into one guy's shin. When he let her go to clutch his leg, she wrenched herself free from the other guy and followed up with a searing blow to the side of the injured guy's head. Then another rapid jab to his abdomen. He crumpled, gasping for breath.

She lunged for the gun, grabbing it from the ground. Without a pause `she hauled off and threw it.` It traced a high arc through the sky. She didn't have time to watch where it landed.

She faced the last one now. He was familiar to her from another time, but her head was too blurry to cobble together a memory. His lips were swollen, and his jacket was speckled with blood, probably hers. Gray spots grew and multiplied, clouding her vision. `She heard the punch to her shoulder before she felt it.` She stepped back and shook her head in the hope of clearing it. She came forward and cracked her fist across his nose. His fist landed hard on her cheekbone. She reeled back, losing her footing, almost falling directly onto Sam.

On your feet, girl, she begged herself. But then she heard something. It was faint but approaching fast and sounded to her more beautiful than a Mozart symphony. The guy heard it, too. He stopped. Listened. He gave her a last look before he ran.

Bless you, Renny, she thought as she fell back against Sam, listening to the siren coming near.

She turned as gingerly as she could. She put her hand on Sam's chest. *He was breathing.* He definitely was. She put her hand gently on his cheek, then skimmed her fingers over his battered eye. She smoothed his hair back from his beautiful forehead. She hadn't touched another human being like this in almost five years. Transfixed, she ran her trembling hand from the cool softness of his upper cheek to the masculine stubble of his chin. His perfect skin was broken in several places. *What had she done to him?*

And almost more disturbing, what had he done to her?

Tears spilled from her eyes and mixed with the blood drying on her face. A drop of the pink moisture landed on his forehead. And another. It blended with the beads of sweat on his brow.

She felt like she was entering a trance as she lowered her face toward his. She touched her lips against his with *exquisite gentleness,* slowly deepening the kiss as she surrendered her heart.

She heard voices coming near. She lifted her head. Sam's eyes fluttered open and then closed again.

She could die now. She laid her head on his chest and melted away.

To: L

From: ELJ

Date: October 2

File: 776244

Subject: Gaia Moore

Last Seen: Washington Square Park, New York City, 8:37 P.M.

Update: Subject hospitalized after prolonged fight with several gang members and a man identified as Sam Moon, age 20, sophomore at NYU. Three gang members arrested at the scene, two others fled. Old man known as Zolov was taken to the hospital and treated for a surface wound to the face. Subject received surface wound to the head, resulting in considerable loss of blood. Multiple contusions. Expected discharge 10/3.

To: ELJ

From: L

Date: October 2

File: 776244

Subject: Gaia Moore

Unacceptable. Subject was not to be injured *under any circumstances*. Contact me immediately for new placement.

When he was near her, his own mind betrayed him.

dangerous hope

The smartest thing he could do was stay away from her permanently.

Boy Flowers

"IT'S SO TRENDY, ALMOST BLEEDING to death. All the cool girls are doing it."

Gaia didn't open her eyes. Instead she considered the voice, felt the calloused hand wrapped around hers. She meant to smile, but it came out wobbly. "Hi, Ed," she said.

When she opened her eyes, she saw a small bundle of orange carnations perched in a Snapple bottle on the bedside table. "Those are such boy flowers," she noted in a weak, slightly raspy voice.

"What do you mean?"

"Only a boy would buy dyed carnations," she explained. "Girls buy less obvious stuff, like tulips and irises."

"Are you saying you don't like them?"

"No, I do like them. I accept that you are a boy. I'm happy that you are a boy."

Ed looked happy that he was a boy, too.

"So who did you beat up this time?" he asked.

"That sounded like a question," she said.

"Oh, yeah. This is like reverse *Jeopardy.* Um . . . let's see. . . . You beat up ten guys, each four times your size, and one poor bastard got in a lucky punch."

She nodded. "Pretty much. Only multiply the equation by one-half."

"Only five guys." He shook his head. "You're losing your edge."

Gaia studied his face thoughtfully. "I guess you could say it was six guys—only one was kind of a mistake."

"A mistake."

"I got in a fight by accident with Sam—Heather's boyfriend."

"Wow, you really do get around."

"I didn't mean to. I thought he'd slashed Zolov, the old guy who plays chess in the park. But it turned out Sam was only trying to help."

"I see. But you discovered that *after* you knocked his head off." He made an obvious effort not to let the end of his sentence bend into a question.

"Sort of," she admitted.

"Mmmm. Maybe you'll find an excuse to beat up Heather's parents next."

"Ha-ha-ha."

Gaia closed her eyes. Her right cheekbone was throbbing, the cut on her forehead stung, and her stomach muscles ached. She was suddenly too tired to think.

"Hey, Ed," she finally said.

"Yup."

"Thank you for trying to be my friend."

"Am I succeeding? Uh . . . I mean . . ." He cleared his throat. "I am succeeding." He said it in a deep, smooth voice, like a news anchor.

She laughed. "Annoyingly well."

He squeezed her hand. "I'm glad."

She moved her toes under the stiff sheets. "Is Heather still in the hospital?" she asked.

Ed nodded. "Two doors down."

"You're joking."

"No, they moved her out of the ICU. She's going home tomorrow, just like you. Maybe you two can have a joint party."

Gaia sighed. "I still need to apologize to her."

"I don't see why."

"For almost getting her killed," Gaia said.

"But that wasn't your fault."

"Yes, it was."

"It wasn't."

"Was."

"Wasn't."

"Was."

"Wasn't."

"Was."

Ed let out his breath in frustration. "Gaia."

"What?"

"You have got to get over yourself."

"What do you mean?"

"Not everything bad that happens has to be about you."

For no reason that she could understand, tears flooded Gaia's eyes. Something big grew in her throat that prevented her from swallowing. Ed was getting close to a place that hurt, and she wanted him to go away. She tipped back her head so the tears wouldn't spill over her bottom lids. Thank the Lord for water cohesion.

Ed watched her carefully. His expression was gentle but serious. "You're tough as hell, Gaia, but you're not a god. You're made of the same stuff as the rest of us."

"Ed?" she asked in a thick voice. "Would you leave now? I think I can only handle having a friend in five-minute bursts."

ZOLOV WAS IN ROOM 502. HEATHER

Remember Heather

was now in room 724, and Gaia was in room 728. Sam had been released from the emergency room last night after being examined and bandaged. He had slept—or at least lain—in his own bed most of last night. Today he made his rotations like a physician. Like a disoriented, exhausted, overwrought, inept physician who hadn't actually gone to medical school.

He had no idea what happened last night. It was a complete mystery why he wasn't dead and who'd fought off the gang. One of the policemen thought it was Renny, the kid who'd called 911, but that didn't make much sense. One of the paramedics jokingly suggested it was Superman.

Sam had this strange, hazy memory of Gaia . . . but no. That was obviously a fitful hallucination—a product of his own deranged fantasy life.

Zolov's slashing wound was minor, but he was so old, the doctor on call wanted to observe him for another twenty-four hours. Zolov seemed to Sam in happy spirits and was very fond of the hospital food. He'd already discovered an orderly who loved to play chess.

Heather lay in the bed only a foot away from him, almost good as new and being released the following afternoon.

Gaia, he hadn't actually spoken to. He'd only prowled around the door to her room like a cat burglar, wanting to catch a glimpse of her but feeling too weird to actually enter.

"So Carrie told me that Miles and them are all coming over tomorrow night. It was supposed to be a surprise, but . . . you know."

Sam didn't know, but he nodded, anyway. Heather had been chatting gaily at him for almost an hour. She was propped up in her bed, surrounded by at least a billion flowers, wearing her own pink linen robe. The bouquet he'd carefully chosen was hidden behind two veritable towers of greenery and a gargantuan basket of fruit. Nurses and doctors and scores and scores of visitors slipped in and out, attending to her as if she were a reigning queen. Her face was flushed and lovely.

"And you'll be there, right?"

Sam glanced up. He'd forgotten to listen to the first part of the question. He nodded again.

"Great. I mean, my mom is going to, like, shit if I'm not in bed by ten. But it will be fun, anyway."

Heather didn't know Gaia was just down the hall. She'd accepted his explanation for his swollen purple eye with a minimum of questions. She'd cooed about how brave he was and how `he'd avenged her`, which wasn't true, of course, but whatever.

". . . Don't you think?" She was looking at him expectantly after a long soliloquy on something or other.

Sam nodded, grateful Heather only asked yes or no questions and rhetorical ones at that.

"I figure we can just order more if we run out," Heather continued.

How had Heather managed to turn a hospital stay into such a social whirlwind? he wondered as two more random friends waved at her from the doorway. "We'll come back," one of them whispered loudly in a `we're-cool-to-the-fact-that-your-boyfriend-is-here` kind of way.

"Right," he said absently.

He was thinking about whether or not the door to room 728 would be fully open and what he might say if he did venture into room 728. And then he felt ashamed. What kind of asshole obsessed about a troubling near stranger when his girlfriend was in the hospital?

He was considering this when Heather's face changed distinctly. He turned to see why. He clamped his jaw down so hard, he nearly crushed his back teeth.

"Um, hello?" It was Gaia hovering at the door. Her face was tentative. He'd never seen her hair down before. It was a pale, beautiful yellow, and there was lots of it—it fell below her shoulders. Her few freckles stood out in the fluorescent light.

Heather's expression turned from surprised to pinched and angry. "What are you doing here?"

"I—I—um, actually spent the night down the hall because—"

Heather shook her head in disbelief. "I swear to God, it's like you're stalking me."

Gaia looked desperately uncomfortable as her gaze shifted from Heather to Sam and then back again. Her skin looked so pale, it was almost translucent. She tugged and fidgeted with her grayish purple hospital gown. "I don't know if you heard, but I . . . there was . . . this fight last night and . . ."

"Do I care?" Heather's voice was so harsh, Sam winced inwardly.

"No, it's just . . ." Gaia sighed and started over. "It doesn't matter. I just wanted to tell you that I'm very sorry for not warning you about the guy with the knife in the park. It was a bad and dishonorable thing to do, and I don't need you to say it's okay or anything. I'm not looking to be friends. But what I did was wrong, and I'm very sorry for it."

Sam's heart moved up through his chest and into his throat as he watched Gaia. He saw something in her eyes (when he let himself) that was so profoundly vulnerable and scarred that her defiance only made it more moving and distressing to him. Was he the only one who saw it? Was he imagining it? He found himself hoping with unfamiliar passion that Heather would be kind to her. Gaia's speech was met with at least a minute of silence.

"Are you done?" Heather finally asked.

Sam's heart dislocated his tonsils. He couldn't swallow. He was supposed to be on Heather's side. She was his girlfriend, and furthermore, she was the one who'd been wronged. But he struggled against the impulse to put his arms around Gaia and tell Heather to go to hell.

Gaia nodded.

"Then please go away," Heather said. She was capable of causing hypothermia when she felt like it.

Gaia left just as Heather's mom arrived in the

doorway. Sam practically leaped to his feet. "Heather, your mom probably wants some time with you," he mumbled, needing to get out of that room if he was ever going to breathe again. "Hey, Mrs. Gannis," he said politely, bolting past her.

He paused for a moment or two before following Gaia into her room. Although it was only a matter of thirty feet from Heather's, it belonged to a different universe. Aside from a pitiful clump of bright orange flowers in a sticky-looking glass bottle, it was colorless, empty, quiet. Gaia was sitting with her arms around her knees on the radiator under the window, staring out at the rain.

"Gaia?" he said.

She turned around. She had those eyes again. "Hi."

She looked like a waif in her hospital gown. Her feet were bare, her ankles surprisingly delicate. Her toenails were mostly covered in chipped brown polish. She had such a big presence, he'd never realized how slight she could appear.

It was too quiet. He needed to say something to her, but the feelings stirring in his core weren't getting anywhere near his mouth. He found his legs taking steps that brought him close to her.

"How are you doing?" she asked softly, filling a tiny part of the silence.

"Oh, fine," he said, as if that were a surprising question. "What about you?"

"Fine. I'm going home tomorrow."

"I'm glad."

He shifted his weight from one foot to the other. "So, where are your folks?"

Her pupils seemed to dilate, but she didn't look away. "I don't have any."

Sam wanted to slit his throat. And yet somehow the information didn't completely surprise him. "I'm so sorry. I didn't mean—"

"That's okay," she said quickly. "How could you have known?"

"I—I didn't . . . I—I just . . ." His voice petered out. So much for the speech therapist.

"Sam," she said.

His name sounded different than it ever had before. "Yes?"

"I am very, very sorry for attacking you last night. I wish I had it to do over."

For some odd reason, he found himself smiling a little. That was the one thing in his life he would have left just the same. "No, no. It wasn't your fault. I'm the one who's sorry . . . for . . . for everything."

"I seem to have a lot to apologize for," she said quietly, studying her fingernails. Her hands were exceptionally graceful, although her nails were bitten down to the quick.

"Some people do, and they say nothing," he murmured. He hoped she would know what he meant.

She nodded.

"Gaia, do you have any idea what happened last night?"

She tilted her head. "What do you mean?"

"I mean, somebody beat up those guys and . . . saved my skin. Maybe yours, too. Do you have any idea who it was or how it happened?"

Her eyes didn't move from his. She was looking for something from him as intently as he was from her. "Probably no more than you," she said equivocally.

He took a deep breath. "I have these strange fragments of memories, but . . . well . . ." He found his cheeks warming at the images in his mind. "But they don't make sense."

Gaia shrugged. "Oh."

"I mean, you didn't . . ." His voice was obviously beseeching, but he couldn't supply the rest of the question.

She wasn't going to help him.

"Maybe it will come back to one of us," he said lamely.

"Maybe."

He stuck his hands in his pants pockets. "Did you see Zolov today?"

Gaia smiled. "Yeah. He's happy. He keeps asking for more pudding."

Sam smiled, too. Suddenly he wanted to stay here and smile at her for the rest of his life.

"Yeah," he repeated stupidly.

She lifted up her arm to brush a strand of hair from her face and as she did revealed a deep, prune-colored bruise on the tender underside of her arm. "Oh," he said out loud, his breath catching. Suddenly he wasn't just close to her but nearly touching her. Two of his fingers hovered around her elbow.

She lifted her arm again and glanced at the bruise, wondering at his reaction. "This?" She turned out her arm and offered it to him.

For some reason the dark, angry bruise on her soft, sweet skin pained him beyond words. It was a helpless spot, even on Gaia's body. She has no parents, he found himself thinking disconnectedly. She has a terrible bruise on that hidden, sad part of her arm and she has no parents.

Without thinking properly, he let his fingertips land on her skin just above the inside of her elbow. Gaia looked down at them, but she didn't flinch. Together they watched his fingers slowly graze the damaged spot so gently, he wasn't sure whether he felt her skin or simply her warmth.

The warmth radiated up into his face, now bent over her. He was hypnotized by that passage of skin. He inhaled her subtle fragrance—a faint but tantalizing mixture of chamomile and Chap Stick and caramel and faded laundry detergent.

Was he breathing? Was his heart still beating?

"It's nothing much," she said in something just above a whisper. "You should see the ones on my stomach."

Oh, God. The mere thought of her stomach was a mistake.

"And this," she said. She lifted a curtain of gold hair to show a nasty bruise on her hairline just above her ear.

Now his hand was on her hair. He'd first realized it last night, that her hair was magical stuff. It was weightless and sparkled with strangely mutable color—as if it were shot through with sunlight.

His eyes were on her wound, then suddenly his lips. It had nothing to do with thinking. If it had anything to do with thinking, he never would have done it. Because he was a cautious, rational person. Everyone said so.

His lips touched her hairline so tenderly. She breathed into him, letting her head, her body relax against him. She let out a tiny sound. A hum, not a word.

He'd found his purpose with her, in that touch of his lips, in those few seconds. Without caution or anything related to reason, he knew (he didn't know how he knew) that he had a unique power. He alone had it. Did she know? Did she care? Would she hate him for it? Or would she, could she, love him?

As his lips moved with exquisite gentleness from

the bruise in her hairline to the bandaged cut over her left eyebrow, he knew that he somehow possessed the power to kiss her and make her better. It was a puzzling, inexplicable kind of certainty that came only in dreams. It was an idea so complex and fragile that if he even blinked, he feared he would lose it.

Let me show you, he thought as his lips moved toward hers. *Let me show you what I can do.*

She was staring up at him in wonder. Her fingers had wrapped around his. Her breath was slow and just barely audible. Her lips were parted in a question. Her blue-violet eyes opened into a billion possible worlds.

"There you are!" The booming words cut through the spell with the force of an ax.

The pretty, plump nurse who'd spoken them was carrying only a paper cup and some pills. "There you are!" she said again, this time clearly to him. Her voice was so loud, it was disorienting. Sam wished he had a remote control to pause her or at the very least turn down the volume.

"You're *Heather's boyfriend, right?*"

Could they hear her all the way uptown? he wondered absently.

"She's *looking for you*—asking *everybody* where *you went.*"

Could they hear her in Harlem? In Connecticut? At the North Pole?

Sam had traveled deep into a netherworld, and it

was hard coming back. He looked at Gaia, but her face was turned to the window.

"Gaia?"

When she turned back to him, her face was different.

"Yeah?"

"I'll see you later?"

"Sure, maybe," she said.

Her eyes were no longer the color of the clear night sky soaring up into a universe of stars and moons and planets and galaxies. They were iced over. Shut.

"Hey, Sam," she called as he walked toward the door.

He felt something dangerous as he turned to her.

"You and Heather make a great couple," she said. Her voice was as frigid as her expression.

All hope and warmth drained away. He blinked.

"I'm not sure how to take that," he said.

She shook her head. "It doesn't matter."

Sam's sore muscles tightened. He pulled his eyes from her face and forced the fuzzy clouds in his mind apart, letting in the cold light of reason.

He was awake. He was fully awake, and the dream was gone. Now he could remember that he disliked Gaia. Even hated her. She was trouble. Within a week of meeting her he'd been beaten to a pulp and two people he really cared about were in the hospital. Gaia was angry and dangerous. When he was near her, his own mind betrayed him. The smartest thing he could do was stay away from her permanently.

The smartest and most rational thing he could do was to get himself back to Heather's room and remember why he loved her.

2 KRISPY KREME DOUGHNUTS

Distraction à la Gaia

1 Granny Smith apple

1 large coffee with milk and 3 sugars

5 roasted nuts

He refused
to look up
and pay her
face any
attention
at all
until
and
finally...
he felt the
metal barrel
against his
temple.

Good-bye, Marco

SHE WAS SO ANGRY, SHE'D PICKED a fight with George. She was so angry, she was wearing her highest heels. Even her aqua miniskirt wasn't helping her mood.

Marco put his hands on her hips and pushed her against the wall.

The only thing the stupid, vain kid had going for him was his looks, and now he was monstrous with his swollen nose and misshapen lips.

"Come on, darling," she whispered to him. "We need some privacy." She removed his hands and used them to lead him down the narrow hall of the Gramercy Inn to room 402, their very own love nest.

Once he was in the room, she plucked the Do Not Disturb sign off the inside doorknob and hung it on the outside. She closed the door hard and locked it. She clattered the key down on the glass-topped bureau.

He was already pulling his cotton T-shirt over his head. She saw deep bruises on his ribs and shoulder. Slob that he was, he threw the shirt on the ground and came toward her with those inexhaustible hands.

"Darling," she cooed, "you know I need to talk to you. I asked you not to hurt my friend, and now I've learned she's in the hospital."

Marco, as usual, was in no mood for talking.

"Mmmm," he said, burying his face in her neck.

This had been fun two days ago. Today it wasn't.

"Marco, did you hear me?"

He had the unbelievable gall to throw her on the bed. She took her handbag with her. As he kissed her, she fumbled with the latch and opened it.

"Marco, I asked you a question."

His hands were gliding under her shirt. They were cold today.

He refused to look up and pay her face any attention at all until he felt the `metal barrel against his temple.` His eyes grew round, and his lips opened. He spluttered but couldn't find words.

Ella gave him another few seconds to fully appreciate her change of mood before she pulled the trigger and sent a silent bullet deep into his head.

She untangled herself from him and deposited the gun into her slim, square bag. She straightened her clothes and glanced in the mirror. Her lipstick was still perfect. She smiled wide. None on her teeth.

This interlude had done nothing to `quell her anger.` But now it was three o'clock, and Gaia, the true source of her temper, would be home from the hospital. Ella slung her bag over her shoulder, enjoying the weight of the gun, and strode to the door without a backward glance.

She was so tired of that girl.

here is a sneak peek of Fearless™ #2: SAM

GAIA

Tonight, as I sat on the park bench waiting for my head to explode, I had one moment of clarity in which I learned two things.

I have to find my dad.

I just have to. As angry as I am, as much as I hate him for abandoning me on the most awful, vulnerable day of my life, I don't want to die without seeing him one more time. I don't know what I will say to him. But there is something I want to know, and I feel like if I can look in his eyes—just for a moment—I'll know what his betrayal meant and whether there is any love or trust, even the possibility of it between us.

And, two I have to have sex.

Oh, come on. Don't act so shocked. I'm seventeen years old. I know the rules about being safe. If my life weren't in very immediate jeopardy, maybe I would let it wait for the exact right time. But let's face it, I may not be around next week, forget about happily ever after. Besides, I have been through a lot of truly awful things in my life, so why should I die without getting to experience one of the few great ones?

Who am I going to have sex with?

Do you have to ask?

All right, I have an answer. In my moment of clarity, the face I saw belonged to Sam Moon. Granted, he hates me. Granted, he has a girlfriend. Granted, his girlfriend hates me even more. But I'll find a way. 'Cause he's the one. I can't say why, he just is.

I wish I could convince myself that CJ wouldn't make good on his threat. But I heard his voice. I saw his face. I know he'll do any crazy thing it takes. Am I afraid? No. I'm never afraid. But the way I see it, dying without knowing love would be a tragedy.

She hated
that pale
blond hair,
a color
you
rarely saw

beauty
and
hideousness

on a person
over the age
of three.

A Precious Ritual

"YOU SOUND WEIRD."

"How do you mean?" Gaia asked.

"I don't know. You just do. You're talking fast or something."

Ed Fargo was honest with Gaia and Gaia was honest with Ed. He appreciated that about their relationship. With most girls he knew, girls like Heather, there were many mystifying levels of bullshit. With Gaia he could just tell her exactly what he was thinking.

Well, actually, not *everything* he was thinking. There was a certain category of thing he couldn't tell her about. That's why it was often easier talking with her on the phone, because when he couldn't see her, which meant he had fewer of those thoughts he couldn't tell her about.

"I almost got shot in the head a little while ago. That's probably why," Gaia suggested.

Ed made a sound somewhere between laughter and choking on a chicken bone. "What?"

That was another thing he appreciated about Gaia. She was always surprising. Though too often in an upsetting way.

Gaia let out her breath. "Oh, God. Where to start. You know that guy CJ?"

"The one who slashed Heather? Isn't he in jail?" Ed asked with a sick feeling in his stomach.

"I guess he got out on bail or something," Gaia said matter-of-factly. "Anyway, CJ's friend Marco is dead, and he thinks I killed him."

Ed groaned out loud. How had his life taken such a turn? Before he met Gaia, he wouldn't have believed he would have a conversation like this.

"Marco is dead, huh? Do you know who did it?"

"Uh-uh. Do you?"

"Gaia!"

"What? Just asking."

Ed clenched the portable phone between his ear and his neck and rolled his wheelchair from his room down the hallway of his family's small apartment and into the galley kitchen. His late evening phone conversations with Gaia had become as precious a ritual as his eleven o'clock milk shake.

"Come on," Ed prodded, hoisting himself up a few inches with his arms to reach the ice cream in the freezer. "Tell me what happened."

"Okay. I was sitting in the park minding my own business—"

"Eating doughnuts," Ed supplied.

"Yes, Ed, eating doughnuts, when that loser came up from behind and shoved a gun into my neck."

"Jesus."

"I didn't take it seriously at first. But it turns out this guy is half-crazed and deadly serious."

"So what happened?" Ed asked, milk shake momentarily forgotten.

Gaia sighed. "He actually pulled the trigger. I thought I was dead—a wild experience, by the way. It turned out he must have loaded the gun in a hurry, because there was no bullet in at least one of the chambers. I took that opportunity to throw him."

"Throw him?"

"You know, like flip him." She was very casual about it.

"Oh, right. Of course," Ed said.

"You're making fun of me again," Gaia said patiently.

Ed shook his head in disbelief. "I'm not, Gaia. It's just . . ." He laughed. "You blow my mind."

"Well, speaking of, I think this guy CJ is dead-set on killing me. I'm scared he's really going to do it," Gaia said.

"You're scared?" Ed asked. Gaia's voice was grave, but he couldn't help feeling it would take more than a pimply white supremacist with a borrowed gun to hurt Gaia. It would take something more on the order of a hydrogen bomb.

"Figure of speech. I'm scared *abstractly*," Gaia explained.

He could hear her thumping her heel against her metal desk. He resumed his milk shake making.

PrrrrrrrRRRRR.

"Ed! I hate when you run the blender when we're talking," Gaia complained loudly.

"Sorry," he said. By the time she finished complaining, the milk shake was perfectly frothy and smooth. That was part of the ritual.

"I don't want to die," she said resolutely. "You know why?"

"Why?" he asked absently, sucking down a huge mouthful of vanilla shake.

"I haven't had sex yet."

Ed spluttered the mouthful all over his dark blue T-shirt. Cough cough cough. "What?"

"I don't want to die before I've had sex."

Cough cough.

"Right," he said.

"So I need to have sex in the next couple of days, just in case," Gaia added.

Cough cough cough cough cough cough cough cough cough cough—

"Ed? Are you okay? Ed? Is somebody around to give you the Heimlich?"

"N-No," Ed choked out. "I'm (cough cough) fine."

In fact, he had about four ounces of milk shake puddled in his lung. Could you die of that? Could you drown by breathing in a milk shake? And shit, he'd like to have sex in the next couple of days, too. (Cough cough cough.)

"Ed, are you sure you're okay?"

"Yesss," he answered in a weak and gravelly voice.

"So, anyway, I was thinking I better do it soon."

"It?"

"Yeah, it. You know, IT."

"Right. It." Ed felt faint. Milk shake, as it turned out, was much less handy in your veins than, say, oxygen, for instance. "So, who . . . uh . . . are you going to do IT with? Or are you just going to walk the streets soliciting people randomly?"

"Ed!" Gaia sounded geniunely insulted.

"Kidding," he said feebly.

"You don't think anybody's going to want to have sex with me, do you?" Gaia sounded hurt and petulant at the same time.

"Mmrnpha." The noise Ed made didn't resemble an English word. It sounded like it had come from the mouth of a nine-month-old baby.

"Huh?"

"I . . . um . . ." Ed couldn't answer. The truth was, although she made every effort to hide it, Gaia was possibly the most beautiful girl he had ever seen in his life—and that was including the women in the Victoria's Secret catalogue, the *SI* swimsuit issue, and that show about witches on the WB. Any straight guy with a live pulse and a thimbleful of testosterone would want to have sex with Gaia. But what was Ed going to say? This was *exactly* the category of conversation he couldn't have honestly with Gaia.

"Anyway, I do know who I'm going to do it with," Gaia said confidently.

"Who?" Ed felt his vision blurring.

"I can't say."

Ed definitely wasn't taking in enough oxygen. Good thing he was in a chair, because otherwise he'd be lying on the linoleum.

"Why can't you say?" he asked, trying to sound calm.

"Because it's way too awkward," Gaia said.

Awkward? Awkward. What did that imply? Could it mean . . . ? Ed's thoughts were racing. Would it be too crude to point out at this juncture that, though his legs were paralyzed, his nether regions were in excellent working condition?

He felt a tiny tendril of hope winding its way into his heart. He beat it back. "Gaia, don't you think you'll need to get past *awkwardness* if you really plan to be doing IT with this person in the next forty-eight hours?"

"Yeah, I guess." She slammed her heel against the desk. "But I still can't tell you."

"Oh, come on, Gaia. You have to."

"I gotta go."

"Gaia!"

"I really do. Cru-Ella needs to use the phone."

"Gaia! Please? Come on! Tell."

"See ya tomorrow."

"Gaia, who? Who who who?" Ed demanded.

"You," he heard her say, in a soft voice, before she hung up the phone.

But as he lay the phone on the counter he knew who'd said the word, and it wasn't Gaia. It was that wretched, misguiding, leechlike parasite called hope.

Freakishly Needy

THE TIME HAD COME. HEATHER GANNIS felt certain of that as she slammed her locker door shut and tucked the red envelope into her book bag. She waited for the deafening late afternoon crowd to clear before striking out toward the bathroom. She didn't feel like picking up the usual half-dozen hangers-on desperate to know what she was doing after soccer practice.

Okay, time to make her move. She caught sight of Melanie Young in her peripheral vision, but pretended she hadn't. She acted as though she didn't hear Tannie Deegan calling after her. Once in the bathroom she hid in the stall for a couple of minutes to be sure she wasn't being followed.

Heather usually liked her high visibility and enormous number of friends, but some of these girls were so freakishly *needy* some of the time. It was like if they missed one group trip to the Antique Boutique they would never recover. Their clinginess made it almost impossible for Heather to spend one private afternoon with her boyfriend.

Heather dumped her bag in the mostly dry sink and stared at her reflection. She wanted to look her best when she saw Sam. She bent her head so close to the mirror that her nose left a tiny grease mark on the glass. This close she could see the light freckles splattered across the bridge of her nose and the amber streaks in her light eyes that kept them from being the bona fide true blue of her mother and sisters.

Her pores looked big and ugly from this vantage point. Did Sam see them this way when he kissed her? She pulled away. She got busy rooting through her bag for powder to tame the oil on her forehead and nose and hopefully cover those gaping, yawning pores. She applied another coat of clear lip gloss. *For somebody who was supposed to be so beautiful, she sure felt pretty plain sometimes.*

She wished she hadn't eaten those potato chips at lunch. She couldn't help worrying that the difference between beauty and hideousness would come down to one bag of salt-and-vinegar chips.

As she swung her bag over her shoulder and smacked open the swinging door, she caught sight of the dingy olive-colored pants and faded black hooded sweatshirt of Gaia Moore. Heather's heart picked up pace and she felt blood pulsing in her temples.

God, she hated that girl. She hated the way she walked, the way she dressed, the way she talked. She hated that pale blond hair, a color you rarely saw on a person over the age of three. Heather wished the color were fake, but she knew it wasn't.

Heather hated Gaia for dumping scorching-hot coffee all over her shirt a couple of weeks ago and not bothering to apologize. Heather hated Gaia for being friends with Ed Fargo, her ex-boyfriend, and turning him against Heather at that awful party. Heather *really* hated Gaia for failing to warn Heather that there was a guy with a knife in the park, when Heather was obviously headed there.

All of those things were unforgivable. But none of them kept Heather up at night. The thing that kept her up at night was one small, nothing comment made by her boyfriend, Sam Moon.

It happened the day Heather got out of the hospital. Sam was there visiting, as he was throughout those five days. He had disappeared for a few minutes and when he got back to her room, Heather asked him where he'd been. He said, "I ran into Gaia in the hallway." That was all. Afterward, when Heather quizzed him, Sam instantly claimed to dislike Gaia. Like everybody else, he said it was partly Gaia's fault that Heather got slashed in the first place.

But there was something about Sam's face when he said Gaia's name that stuck in Heather's mind and would not go away.

Heather's mind flashed again on the card floating in her bag. She sorted through the bag and pulled it out. She needed to check again that the words seemed right. That the handwriting didn't look too girly and stupid. That the phrasing didn't seem too . . . desperate.

She'd find Sam in the park playing chess with that crazy old man, as he often did on Wednesday afternoons. And if not, she'd go on to his dorm and wait for him there. She'd hand him the card, watch his face while he read it, and kiss him so he'd know she meant it.

She was in love with Sam. This Saturday marked their six-month anniversary. He was the best-looking, most intelligent guy she knew. She loved the fact that he was in college.

She had made this decision with her heart. Sam was sexy. Sam was even romantic sometimes. She wanted him to be the one.

So why, then, as she wrote the card, was she thinking not of Sam, but of Gaia?

Dear Sam,

These last six months have been the best of my whole life. Sorry to be corny, but it's true. So I wanted to celebrate the occasion with a VERY special night. I'll meet you at your room at 8 on Saturday night and we'll finally do something we've been talking about doing for a long time. I know I said I wanted to wait, but I changed my mind.

You are the one and NOW is the time.

Love and kisses (all over),
Heather

OFFICIAL RULES FOR
"WIN A $1,000 SHOPPING SPREE AT ALLOY.COM"

NO PURCHASE NECESSARY. Sweepstakes begins October 1, 1999 and ends November 30, 1999. Entrants must be 14 years or older as of October 1, 1999 and a U.S. legal resident to enter. Corporate entities are not eligible. Employees of Alloy Online, Inc., Simon & Schuster, Inc., and 17th Street Productions, their advertising, promotion, production agencies, the affiliated companies of each and the immediate family members (or people living in the same household) of each are not eligible. Participation in this Sweepstakes constitutes contestant's full and unconditional agreement to and acceptance of the Official Sweepstakes Rules.

HOW TO ENTER: To enter, visit the Alloy Web site at www.alloy.com. Submit your entry by fully completing the entry form at the site. Entries must be received by November 30, 1999, 11:59 pm Eastern Standard Time. There is no charge or cost to register. No mechanically reproduced entries accepted. One entry per e-mail address. Simon & Schuster, Inc. and Alloy Online, Inc. and their respective agents are not responsible for incomplete, lost, late, damaged illegible or misdirected e-mail for technical, hardware or software failures of any kind, lost or unavailable network connections, or failed, incomplete garbled or delayed computer transmissions which may limit a user's ability to participate in the Sweepstakes. All notifications in the Sweepstakes will be sent by e-mail. We are not responsible, and may disqualify you if your e-mail address does not work or if it is changed without prior notice to us via e-mail at contest@alloymail.com. Sponsor reserves the right to cancel or modify the Sweepstakes if fraud or technical failures destroy the integrity of the Sweepstakes as determined by Sponsor, in its sole discretion. If the Sweepstakes is so canceled, any and/or all announced winners will receive prizes to which they are entitled as of the date of cancellation; the unawarded prizes will be donated to charity.

RANDOM DRAWING: Grand, First and Second prize winners will be selected in a random drawing from among all eligible entries on December 1, 1999 to be conducted by Alloy Online designated judges, whose decisions are final. Winners will be notified by e-mail on or about December 3, 1999. Odds of winning a Grand, First or Second prize depends on the number of eligible entries received.

PRIZES:

Grand Prize (1): A One Thousand ($1,000) Dollar online shopping spree of merchandise from Alloy.com. (Approximate retail value - $1,100 including tax and shipping.)

First Prize (1): A Two Hundred Fifty ($250) Dollar online shopping spree of merchandise from Alloy.com (Approximate retail value - $280 including tax and shipping.)

Second Prize (1): A One Hundred ($100) Dollar online shopping spree of merchandise from Alloy.com (Approximate retail value - $115 including tax and shipping.)

All prizes will be awarded within 6-8 weeks of announcement of winners. Prizes are subject to all federal, state and local taxes, which are the sole responsibility of the winners. Prizes are not transferable. No cash substitutions, transfer or assignment of prize will be allowed, except by Sponsor in which case a prize of equal or greater value will be awarded.

GENERAL: All federal, state and local laws and regulations apply. Void in Florida and wherever prohibited. By entering, winners consent to use of their names by Sponsor without additional compensation. Entries become Sponsor's property and will not be returned. For a copy of these official rules, send a self-addressed stamped envelope to Alloy 115 West 30th Street #210, NY, NY 10001, Attn: $1,000 Shopping Spree Sweepstakes.

AFFIDAVIT OF ELIGIBILTY/RELEASE: To be eligible to win, winners will be required to sign and return an affidavit of eligibility/release of liability (except where prohibited by law). Winners under the age of 18 must have their parent or guardian sign the affidavit and release as well. Failure to sign and return the affidavit or release with 14 days, or to comply with any term or condition in these Official Rules may result in disqualification and the prize being awarded to an alternate winner Return of any prize notification/prize as undeliverable may result in disqualification and the awarding of the prize to an alternate winner. By accepting prizes, winners grant Sponsor permission to use his or her name, picture, portrait, likeness and voice for advertising, promotional and/or publicity purposes connected with this Sweepstakes without additional compensation (except where prohibited by law).

Neither Simon & Schuster, Inc. nor Sponsor shall have responsibility or liability for any injury, loss or damage of any kind arising out of participation in this Sweepstakes or the acceptance or use of the prize.

WINNERS LIST: The winners list and entries will be posted at www.alloy.com on December 10, 1999 or, for a list of prize winners available after December 15, 1999 send a self-addressed, stamped, #10 envelope to: Alloy 115 West 30th Street #201 NY, NY 10001,
Attn: $1,000 Shopping Spree Sweepstakes.